Lazarus

Anonna Reign

Quantum Discovery
A LITERARY AGENCY

ISBN
978-1-961601-53-6 (Paperback)
978-1-961601-54-3 (eBook)
978-1-961601-52-9 (Hardcover)

Lazarus

Table of Contents

Introduction..vii

Chapter 1 1
Chapter 2 4
Chapter 3 10
Chapter 4 15
Chapter 5 20
Chapter 6 25
Chapter 7 30
Chapter 8 36
Chapter 9 43
Chapter 10 53
Chapter 11 62
Chapter 12 66
Chapter 13 71
Chapter 14 77
Chapter 15 81
Chapter 16 88
Chapter 17 95
Chapter 18 99
Chapter 19 104
Chapter 20 110
Chapter 21 117
Chapter 22 120
Chapter 23 124
Chapter 24 128
Chapter 25 135

Introduction

Marcus lie in bed, trying to catch his breath. The cancer had spread all over his body. "Liza!" he called, with tears running down his face. "Liza, I need you." "I'm here, Father," Liza said, trying to fight her tears. "I have to tell you something," Marcus began, "something that I should have told you a long time ago." "Dad, please! You need your strength," Liza pleaded. "No Liza, listen to me," he said, coughing. Liza looked back at the nurse with a worried look on her face. She wanted her father to save his strength. After all, he only had a few days left on earth, according to the doctor's report. Marcus raised his frail little body up and pointed to a picture on his dresser. There in the picture was a very handsome man. "I tried, God!" Marcus said, crying hysterically. "Dad! What is it?" Marcus looked into his daughter's eyes and shook his head, crying. He kept pointing to the picture. "I tried to warn him about the truth," he said. "What truth?" Liza said, confused. "The truth about his eternal soul," Marcus said, crying hard.

.

Chapter 1

It was the beginning of the year, and Julius Willingham was having his normal birthday celebration. Everyone in town was there, from the wealthiest to the middle class. Julius Willingham was the richest man in town. He and his brother John were owners of hotels and restaurants all around the world. Julius was devastatingly handsome. He was well-respected and had the support of lots of family and friends. All the women in the town of Pineville wanted him, but he only had eyes for one woman, Ava Benjamin. Ava was a beautiful black woman. She was tall and slender. Her caramel skin went beautifully with her brown eyes. She had long curly hair that draped down her back. Ava was the daughter of a preacher by the name of Jerry Benjamin. She, her sister, Sissy, and her mother, Marline, lived in a nice home near the city's church. Julius looked around with anticipation for Ava to show up. "If I didn't know better, I would say that you're looking for Ava," a voice behind him said. It was Marcus, Julius' best friend. "Marcus, I'm just simply enjoying my guests," Julius lied. "Un-huh, sure you are," Marcus said, not buying his friend's remark. Just then, Ava and her family arrived. One of the housekeepers escorted her in. She was wearing a beautiful dress that showed off her curves. "Dang, Ava is fine!" John said, joining Julius and Marcus, who were having a staring contest. "I tell you, gentlemen, that's the future Mrs. Julius Willingham," Julius said, not taking his eyes off the tall beauty. "Don't look now Ava, but you have an audience," Sissy said, laughing. Ava turned to look at Julius, who was standing there watching her every move. She then flashed a smile at him and began mingling with the guests. "I hope that's juice," Pastor Benjamin said, teasing one of the guests. "Oh yeah, Pastor, this is definitely juice," a woman name Tara said, holding up her glass where Pastor Benjamin could see. "Yeah, juice with a little taste of gin," Tara whispered to one of her friends, as the Pastor passed by. "Dad, why do you even come to these parties if you intend on sucking out all the fun?" Ava whispered, as she kept waving at guests. "Oh, I'm just making sure they show up to church on Sunday," he said, kissing her on the cheek. Ava looked over and spotted some of her friends. "Hey Dad, I'll meet up with you later," Ava said, walking away. She then went over to join, who her mom loved to call, the "Fashion Divas." It was Lily, Violet, and Sandy, the normal crew who always met together at Mary's. "Hey, you guys!" Ava said, running up to her crew and hugging them. "Girl, don't mess up the hair, it took me an hour fixing it," Violet said, making sure that her hair was still in place. "Girl, you look sensational," Sandy said, looking Ava up and down. "Oh, this old thing," Ava said, laughing. "Hey Ava, if I didn't know any better, I would think you are deliberately ignoring Julius tonight," Lily said, giving her a tiny shove. "Well, I want to see him sweat," Ava said, turning to look at Julius and then back at her friends. They all looked at each other and then started laughing. Julius stared over at the girls and shook his head. "So, Ava's playing the dodging game tonight?" Marcus asked, sipping his wine. "Yeah, well, you know women love playing games," Julius said, pretending not to care. "She sure does drive you wild, doesn't she my friend?" Marcus asked. "More than you know," Julius admitted. "So what are you going to do?" Marcus asked. "I'm going to go and dance with Cindy," Julius said, walking away. "Oh man, you are playing hard ball," Marcus said, laughing. The girls pretended not to notice Julius when he went over and started talking to Cindy Miller. "What's he doing now?" Ava asked. "Oh, he's dancing with Cindy," Sandy said, looking at them as though they were crazy. Ava turned around and watched as Julius danced with Cindy. She stared at the two and became very angry. She stormed out to the balcony to cool down. "Well, your little plan has worked. She just stormed out," Cindy said, smiling. "Thanks, Cindy," Julius said, kissing her on the cheek. "Anytime!" she said, looking at him from behind as he walked out to confront Ava. Ava looked at Julius and rolled her eyes. "What's wrong, baby?" he asked, as if he didn't already know. "You deliberately tried making me jealous with that piece of trash!" Ava snapped. "So, did it work?" Julius asked, teasing. Ava looked at him with disgust and stormed back into the party. Julius grabbed her arm before she could reach her destination. "Let go, Julius," Ava snapped. "Baby, I'm sorry. I was wrong," he said apologetically. Ava tried not looking into his handsome face. She could not deny that he was as gorgeous as he had ever been. "You hit below the belt, Julius, and embarrassed me in front of my friends," Ava snapped. She was just about to argue some more, but he grabbed her up to him and kissed her. It seemed as if the party stopped when everyone saw Julius kiss Ava so passionately. Even Pastor Benjamin was shocked by his boldness. Sissy snickered to herself, watching their father squirm in his seat. Ava's pulse raced as she looked into Julius' eyes. "I'm sorry, I don't know what came over me," he said, walking away from her. "Julius, wait!" Ava yelled. Julius turned around to face the tall beauty. "I don't want you to go," she admitted. He then walked over to her and began kissing her again. Marcus and John both looked at him as if they were giving him a high five in their thoughts. All the girls' eyes were filled with envy, while Ava's father looked horrified. Sissy continued staring at her father and would snicker to herself. Julius and Ava breathed heavily. "Julius, people are staring at us," Ava said, looking around. "I don't care. Everyone in this town knows how I feel about you," he said, caressing her face. "Ava, I told you, I have never felt this way about any woman, the way that I feel about you," he admitted. Ava grabbed his hand. "Julius, we come from two different worlds and I'm not sure that I fit into your world," Ava confessed. "Ava, don't judge me by the money I have. It's nothing if I can't share it with you." "Julius, you live a life filled with splendor and I don't know if I can handle pressure like that," Ava admitted. "So, what are you saying, Ava?" "I'm just saying that we should continue to get to know each other better," Ava argued. "OK, I'll wait for you. For forever if I have to," he said. He stroked her face again, then turned away from Ava and left the party.

Chapter 2

Marline and Pastor Jerry Benjamin stood at the airport, waiting for Lazarus. "What if he doesn't recognize us?" Marline asked. "He will. Carl had plenty of pictures of us over the years," Jerry assured her. "I feel so bad for Lazarus. Losing his father like that, so sudden, and now the boy has no family," Marline said. "Well, he has us," Jerry said, rubbing his wife's back. Lazarus came walking up and he was the spitting image of his father. The same tanned complexion and beautiful hazel eyes. He wore a thin mustache leading down to a nicely trimmed beard. He stood about 6'3 and had a nice slim, masculine body. "Oh my God! Is that him?" Marline said, holding her hand to her mouth. Lazarus started smiling as he walked up to the Benjamins. "Lazarus, boy, you are so handsome--the spitting image of your father," Marline said, hugging him. "Welcome home, son!" Jerry said, giving him a fist bump.

The trip home was quiet. Jerry wanted to wait until he had Mrs. Benjamin home before he asked Lazarus all the tough questions. He dropped Marline off at the house and headed to the church. "Lazarus, I brought us here to talk," Jerry admitted. "Talk about what?" Lazarus asked. "Your father's last wishes," Jerry said. "He told me already that he wanted you to look after me, but with all due respect Mr. Benjamin, I'm a grown man," Lazarus argued. "I know you are, Lazarus, and I would never try to run your life. I just want to be there for you--the way that Carl would have wanted me to be," Jerry assured him. "Thank you, Mr.

Benjamin, that means a lot." "Hey! I want you to call me Jerry," Jerry said, grabbing his shoulder. "OK, Jerry," Lazarus said, smiling. "Well, we better get you settled. And since you're real crafty with your hands, you'll find no problem getting work in this town." Lazarus nodded his head as Jerry escorted him out. They both jumped into the truck and headed to the house. Right across from the large five-bedroom house that Jerry Benjamin owned was a tiny house. Jerry pulled up to the tiny house, which looked as if it had been abandoned for years. "I know it isn't much, but a little love is all this place needs," Jerry said, making his way through the yard. Lazarus looked around at the big mess. "Hey Lazarus, if it's too much, you can always stay at the house with us. I just assumed you wanted your own space." "It's perfect, Jerry. It's exactly what I need right now," Lazarus said, smiling. Jerry smiled at the young man and opened the front door. "You have a fireplace that keeps this whole place pretty warm during those cold winter nights, and you have tools if you need to fix anything in this closet," Jerry said, fanning a cobweb out of the way. "Also, the water is working really good, but be careful, it gets pretty hot." "Thanks, Jerry, I can take it from here," Lazarus said, trying not to laugh. "Okay. I know I can be a little pushy sometimes. If you need anything, Lazarus, please don't hesitate to come to the house. I mean, if you get hungry or anything," Jerry said, heading out the door. "I will," Lazarus assured him. Lazarus closed the door and let out a big sigh. He walked over to the dusty old couch and sat down, burying his face in his hands.

The next morning, Ava tossed and turned, not being able to get the sound of a loud lawnmower out of her head. "What is that?!" she said, rising up out of bed, feeling frustrated. "It's the hot new guy that's staying in the guest house," Sissy said, staring out the window. "What? Why are you in my room?" Ava snapped. "To get a better view," Sissy said, shaking her head. Ava, being irritated with Sissy, got up and stormed over to the window. When she looked out, a glimpse of Lazarus shocked her. He was mowing the lawn without a shirt on. The hot sun glistened off his masculine body. "He is fine, isn't he?" Sissy said, staring at the handsome young man. "So, that's Daddy's friend, the one that's going to be staying with us?" "Yeah, his name is

Lazarus." "You mean Lazarus, like in the bible?" "Yeah. I wonder if he has a little brother," Sissy said, giving Ava a devious look. "Get out of my room," Ava said, looking irritated with her baby sister's last comment. Sissy turned around and flipped her long hair in Ava's face and walked out. After Sissy left out, Ava turned her attention back to the handsome stranger mowing the lawn.

Ava got showered and dressed, and then headed down to the breakfast table. There at the table, her father was reading a newspaper and Sissy was feeding the dog underneath the table. Marline was at the stove, slaving over turkey-bacon and pancakes. Marline was still a beautiful woman. She had long hair that she always wore back in a bun. She had beautiful mocha skin and had a coca-cola figure. Ava walked over to the table and slumped down in her chair. She tried to look away when she noticed her dad staring at her. "What, Dad?" Ava said, annoyed by the disappointing looks he was giving her. "I want to talk about the other night," Jerry said, putting his newspaper down. "What about it?" Ava said, pretending that she didn't know what he was talking about. "About the show that you and Julius put on at the party the other night." "Daddy, he the one kissed me," Ava said, in her own defense. "What?!" Marline said, looking back at the two of them. "Our daughter behaved like a streetwalker," Jerry said, looking at Marline. "Jerry!" Marline said, upset by the words he used to describe their daughter's behavior. "It's okay, Mother, I'm used to his venomous words," Ava said, looking at her father as if she was immune to his behavior. "No daughter of mine goes around behaving the way you did," Jerry fussed. "I am a grown woman, Dad," Ava snapped. "If you are so grown, then get out of my house." "Fine, I will!" Ava got up and stormed out of the house. She ran out so quickly that she didn't see Lazarus coming up. She bumped right into him and fell down. Lazarus looked down at Ava and extended his hand to pick her up. Ava looked up at the handsome stranger who was trying to help her. He was breathtaking. She had never seen a man as handsome as Lazarus before. Not even Julius' good looks and charm, held a candle to Lazarus. Ava grabbed his hand, and with his strength, he picked her up as if she were paper. "Thank you. I mean, I'm sorry for bumping into you," Ava said, apologizing. "It's okay," he said, smiling. "I'm Lazarus." "I'm Ava, Jerry's daughter," Ava said, trying not to look into his gorgeous hazel eyes. "Are you alright?" Lazarus asked. "Yeah, just had a disagreement with my dad, that's all," Ava said, trying to smile. "Well, if you ever want to talk, I'm a good listener," he said, smiling. "I just might take you up on that offer," Ava said, smiling back. "Please do," he said, in a flirty tone. Ava could feel butterflies in her stomach. She was mesmerized by his charm. "Well, I better go," she said, walking off. Lazarus stood there watching Ava get into the car. He couldn't take his eyes off of her.

Julius sat at his desk, catching up with his paper work. "Julius, you have a visitor," Marcus said, coming in. "Marcus, I told you that I don't want to be bothered," Julius said, not taking his eyes off of his work. "Okay, I'll tell Ava to come back," Marcus said, walking towards the door. "Ava! Ava's here?" Julius said, getting up. "Yes she is, and may I add, she's looking hot," Marcus said, shaking his head. "Well, send her in," Julius said. Ava let herself in, and before Julius could say anything, she walked up to him and hugged him. "What's wrong?" he said, looking into her eyes. "I had another fight with my father," Ava began. Julius kissed her on the forehead and held her tight. "Julius, I don't know what to do. He always acts as if he's disappointed in me," Ava cried. "Baby, why do you put up with it? I tell you over and over to come and stay with me." "Yeah, right, that would definitely send him through the roof, when the town finds out that the preacher's daughter is shacking." "Well, what can I do to make you feel better?" "I don't know," Ava said, walking over to the window. "You know what your problem is, don't you?" Julius said, walking up behind her. "No, what?" Ava said, turning to face him. "You are scared to disappoint your father, and as a result, you find it hard to commit to anything." Ava rolled her eyes in the back of her head. "Ava, it's true. Even when I try getting close to you, you pull away," Julius said, grabbing her face into his hands. "I don't know what to say," Ava said, looking into his eyes. "I want you to say that you will be mine. Ava, I want you to marry me," Julius confessed. "Julius, you can have any woman in this town. Why me?" Ava asked. "I want you Ava, because I love you, and I want to spend the rest of my life with you." Ava put her head down. She was still not ready to commit to Julius. "Look Ava, if you won't marry me, at least act like we have something here. I mean, are we in a relationship or what?" Julius said, confused. "Julius, I want to give you more. I'm just not ready," Ava confessed. Julius stared at her with a disappointed look on his face. "You need to make up your mind, Ava… if you want to be with me or not," he said, storming out. Ava buried her face in her hands, and let out a sigh.

Later that night, Ava lay in bed, thinking about Julius' words. A knock on her bedroom door interrupted her thoughts. "Who is it?" Ava said, rising up. "It's me, Sissy!" "Come in," Ava said, flopping back down on her queen-sized bed. Sissy opened the door and tiptoed in--as if she was trying not to wake up the rest of the house. "Can I sleep with you tonight?" Sissy begged. "Let me guess, you watched a scary movie?" Ava asked. "Zombies On Board," Sissy admitted. "Get in!" Ava said, pulling the covers back and shaking her head. Sissy ran over to the bed, jumped in, and pulled the covers up to her chin. Ava looked at her little sister and laughed. "One of these days, you'll learn," Ava said, giving her an 'I told you so' look. She then began thinking about Julius again. "Ava, why did you skip dinner tonight?" "I had a lot on my mind, that's all," Ava said, hoping her little sister would forget the whole deal and just go to sleep. "Let me guess, man trouble?" Sissy said, sitting up and resting her head on her hand. "What do you know about man trouble?" Ava said, poking her. "I know that Julius is in love with you and you won't commit," Sissy said, nodding her head at her sister. Ava remained quiet. "Oh, I'm sorry, Ava, I didn't mean to upset you." "It's fine. I know it's the talk of the town, that I'm silly for leaving Julius hanging. But the truth is, Sissy…. I don't feel that feeling. You know, that feeling when you can't hardly breathe because that person takes your breath away." "Yes, I know that feeling," Sissy said, gazing up at the ceiling. "I just don't think that Julius is the one," Ava admitted. "Well, you do know that all the women in this town would kill to be in your shoes," Sissy said. "Yes, I know," Ava said. "So, what do you like in a man?" Sissy asked. "Well, for one, I want a man who isn't selfish. You know, a man who thinks more about others than he thinks of himself. And let's just face it, Julius is not that guy. In a crisis, he would probably save himself and forget others around him." "What about Lazarus?" Sissy asked. "Lazarus!" Ava asked, surprised. "Yeah, Lazarus!" "Sissy, I don't even know this Lazarus," Ava argued. "Well, he is fine," Sissy said, shaking her head. "I can't argue with that, but it takes more than good looks to turn my head," Ava assured her. "Well, he joined us for dinner tonight, and I think he is really nice," Sissy confessed. "Is that right?" "Yeah, and plus, he asked about you," Sissy blabbed. "Me?" Ava said, trying not to reveal her excitement. "Yeah, he said that he ran into you in the yard and that you were very beautiful," Sissy confessed. "He said that?" Ava said, smiling. "He sure did," Sissy confessed. Ava turned over and thought about how she felt when she first saw Lazarus. She was definitely captivated.

Chapter 3

The next day, Ava made her way down to the breakfast table. "Good morning, Mother!" she said, kissing her mother on the cheek. "Good morning, Father!" she said, wrapping her arms around him. "OK, what do you want?" Jerry asked. "Nothing, Father, I'm just in a good mood, that's all," Ava said, pouring herself some coffee. Jerry looked at his daughter and then at his wife, confused. Ava sat at the table, thinking about what Sissy had confided in her last night. "So honey, you have a hot date or something?" Marline asked, looking at her husband. "No, why do you say that?" Ava asked, sipping her coffee. "Well, for starters, you're wearing a dress and makeup," Marline pointed out. "No, Mom, I just wanted to feel beautiful today, that's all." Sissy looked at her big sister and smiled. She had a feeling that Ava was dressing to please Lazarus. Marline kept giving her daughter the 'I know what's going on' look, while Jerry sat there clueless. Just then, a knock on the door startled them. Marline looked out of the screen door and saw that it was Lazarus. "Come in, Lazarus," she said, smiling. Lazarus came in. "Hey Lazarus," Jerry said, smiling at the young man. "Come on, sit down and get you some breakfast," Marline fussed. Lazarus sat down right across from Ava. When Ava saw him, she was completely blown away with the handsome stranger. He wore a t-shirt and jeans that went well with his masculine build. Sissy shook her head when she saw the look on her sister's face. "Good morning, Sissy," he said, smiling and pinching her cheek. "Morning Lazarus," Sissy said blushing. "Hello

Ava," he said, looking serious. Ava wanted to melt when she heard his masculine voice call her name. "Hello, Lazarus," Ava said, trying to keep her cool. "Hey Lazarus, I made you pancakes and turkey-bacon, just the way you like it," Marline said, giving him a plate. "Thank you, Mrs. Benjamin," Lazarus said, digging in. "Hey! What did I tell you? Call me Marline," Marline said, hitting him with her pot holder. "Yes ma'am," he said, taking a bite of his food. "So, Lazarus, how did things go at Mrs. Butcher's house?" Jerry asked. "It went OK. She was really pleased with my work," Lazarus said, between bites. "Well that's a surprise…" "Marline," Jerry said, interrupting his wife. "Well, it is! That woman is never satisfied!" Marline argued. "It's spreading all around town, the good work you do. Soon you'll have customers from here to Scotland," Jerry assured him. Just then, the phone rang. "Hello?" Sissy said, grabbing the phone. "Oh, hi Julius," Sissy said. Ava began waving to her sister that she didn't want to talk to him. "Well, Ava's not available right now," Sissy lied. "Sure, I'll tell her," Sissy said, hanging up the phone. "What was that all about?" Jerry asked. "Nothing, Father," Ava said, sipping her coffee. "Is there trouble in paradise?" Jerry asked, not taking his eyes off of his newspaper. "I'm sure you would like that very much," Ava snapped. Lazarus looked at Jerry and then at Ava. The tension in the air was so thick, you could cut it with a knife. Ava tried not to look Lazarus in the face. She felt embarrassed that he had to witness her father's disapproval of her. "Hey, Ava, are you and Sissy still going to the store to meet with your friends?" Marline asked, trying to break the tension. "Yeah!" Ava said, getting up. "Lazarus, didn't you say you needed to go to town to get some tools?" Marline asked. "Yeah!" Lazarus admitted. "Ava, if it's ok with you, can Lazarus ride with you girls?" Marline asked. "Sure," Ava said. Sissy saw an opportunity for Lazarus and Ava to be alone together and she let out a loud groan. "What's wrong with you, Sissy?" Ava asked. "I don't know. I think it's the breakfast. Ava, I'm going to have to take a rain check and go with you some other time," Sissy said, holding her stomach and running out of the kitchen. "Well, I guess that leaves you and me," Ava said, looking at Lazarus. "That's fine with me," Lazarus said smiling.

Ava and Lazarus made their way to the truck. Before Ava could open the door, Lazarus reached over and opened it for her. "Thank you," she said, looking surprised. Ava pulled out of the driveway and started driving towards their destination. She noticed Lazarus checking her out and she just smiled. "So…what do you do around here for fun?" Lazarus asked. "Well, a lot of the people around our age go to Tammy's Jazz Club," Ava said, trying to concentrate on the road. "Is that right?" "Yeah," Ava said, smiling. "What about you, Ms. Ava? What do you like to do?" "Well, I like spending time with my girls, sometimes I like to take long walks on the beach, watch a good horror movie, you know," Ava said, blushing. "Yeah, I know," Lazarus said, smiling. Ava pulled up to the shopping center and parked the truck. "Well, here we are!" she said, turning the truck off. Lazarus got out of the truck and opened the door for her. "Thanks again," she said, getting out. "Well, if you need me, I'll be over at this clothing store," Ava said, pointing to a shop filled with women's clothes. "OK," Lazarus said, smiling. When he smiled, Ava found herself staring. "Well, I'll see you in a little bit," she said, walking away. Ava walked in, just in time to catch her two friends staring out the window at Lazarus. "You two are pathetic," Ava said, shaking her head. "Ava…who is that?" Lily asked. "His name is Lazarus and he's staying in our family's guesthouse. "Oh yeah, I heard of him, he's the talk around town," Violet said. "What talk?" Ava asked. "You know…how good-looking he is and how he's good with his hands." "Girl, I bet he is good with those hands," Lily said, shaking her head. Ava rolled her eyes in the back of her head, irritated by her friend's remark. Violet noticed the look that Ava gave Lily and got suspicious. "So, Ava…you haven't tried to scoop that?" Violet asked. "What? No," Ava said, trying to sound convincing. "Well, I guess you wouldn't mind me going after him," Violet said, testing her. "Well, I heard through the grapevine that he has a girlfriend already," Ava lied. "Really?" Violet said, looking at Lily. "I think she's lying. I think she has the hots for him!" Lily said. "Well, you can think what you want," Ava snapped. Lily looked at Violet and shook her head. "Ava, we know that tone," Violet assured her. "What tone?" Ava asked. "The tone that says, 'you guys are right and you are on to me'," Lily said. "Will you guys just leave it alone?" Ava snapped. "Why should we? It's obvious that something's bothering you," Violet said. "I'm smitten with him," Ava mumbled. "Did I hear what I think I heard?" Lily asked. "Yes, okay, ever since I ran into Lazarus, I can't get him off my mind," Ava blurted out. When she looked at the expressions on her friends' faces, she knew that they weren't alone. Ava looked back to find Lazarus standing there. Ava was so embarrassed. She couldn't believe her eyes. But it was true, Lazarus was standing right there. "Ava, I was just coming in to tell you that I'll be in the truck waiting for you," Lazarus said. He then walked out. "Oh God! Please tell me he didn't just hear me," Ava said, panicking. "Ava, don't worry about it, I'm sure the dude's flattered. I mean, you're beautiful and guys would kill to have you even look their way," Violet said. "Oh God! It's going to be so awkward driving back with him," Ava said, in a nervous wreck. "No, it won't," Lily argued. "Yeah, maybe he'll tell you to pull over on the side of the road and make passionate love to you," Violet suggested. "Violet don't scare her, she's a virgin, for crying out loud." "I wish I had a clone right now," Ava said. She turned to see Lazarus sitting in the truck, waiting patiently. "Hey, from what I learned, the dude is a nice guy. Worst case scenario, he'll probably turn you down in a nice way," Lily said. With that, Ava left and headed for the truck. When Lazarus saw her come out, he jumped out of the truck and opened the door for her.

The ride home was quiet. Ava wondered what Lazarus thought of her after hearing her outburst. Suddenly, they heard a loud sound and Ava swerved off the road. "Are you alright?" Lazarus asked. Ava, still out of breath, nodded her head. Lazarus jumped out of the truck. "We got a flat tire," he said, while examining the situation. "Just great!" Ava said, shaking her head. Lazarus started digging around for a jack. When he found it, he went right to work. Ava got out of the truck to see what the fuss was about. "Ava, I need you to hold these bolts for me," he said, handing her the bolts. Just then, it started pouring down rain. "Oh, just great!" Ava pouted. "It'll be okay, Ava. A little rain won't hurt you," Lazarus said, laughing. Ava stood there, shivering from the cold rain. When Lazarus saw her, he escorted her back inside the truck. "Maybe we should wait until the rain lets up," he said. Ava turned on the heat to warm up a little bit. "Are you alright?" Lazarus asked. "Yes," Ava said, trying to warm up. "I saw a blanket in the back seat," he said, reaching in the back seat to get it. When he put the blanket around her arms, he caught a glimpse of her eyes. He stared intensely into her eyes, as if he wanted to kiss her. Just then, they were startled by a car speeding past, with the horn honking. "It looks like the rain let up. I'd better finish putting the spare on," he said, getting out the truck. Ava waited patiently for Lazarus to get done. Finally, he jumped back into the truck. "It's ready to go," he assured her. On the way to the house, thoughts flooded Ava's mind. She wondered if he wanted to kiss her as much as she wanted to kiss him. She also wondered how he felt about what she said back at the store. She pulled into the driveway and decided to give up on the idea of her and Lazarus. Ava got out of the truck, not waiting for Lazarus to open the door, and headed for the house. She wanted to just go in and forget the day ever happened. "Ava!" Lazarus called. Ava turned around to face the handsome young man. Lazarus walked up to her. "Ava, I just wanted to say that I feel the same way. From the moment I first saw you…I can't get you off my mind. I know you're seeing someone right now, but I know if I didn't tell you how I felt, I would regret it. I was just wondering, or I was hoping, that we could go out sometime?" "I would really like that. Why don't you pick me up tomorrow at six?" Ava said, gazing into his beautiful hazel eyes. "I'll be here," he said, smiling. Lazarus watched as Ava walk into the house. She was definitely the girl of his dreams.

Chapter 4

Ava threw outfit after outfit on her bed, trying to decide what to wear. "I told you, Ava, to wear this one," Sissy said, holding up a red dress. "No, that one makes me look too fat," Ava confessed. "Well what about this black one here?" Sissy said, holding up another dress. "No, that makes me look too skinny," Ava said. Marline walked in. "Mom, please help this girl, she's driving me nuts," Sissy complained. "Why not wear that black and gray dress," Marline suggested. "Now that's a good idea," Ava said, grabbing it out of her closet. When she said that, Sissy threw her arms in the air in frustration.

Meanwhile, Jerry sat on the couch watching TV. He was just about to go into the kitchen when a knock on the door stopped him. A big smile appeared on his face when he opened the door and Lazarus was standing on the other side. "Come on in here, Lazarus!" he said, letting him in. Lazarus walked in and looked around for the rest of the family. "They're upstairs," Jerry explained, as if he was reading Lazarus' thoughts. "Hey Jerry, I hope you don't mind me going out with your daughter," Lazarus asked. "Are you kidding? I'm ecstatic!" he said, putting his arms around him. Lazarus smiled. It meant so much to him, to have Jerry on his side. "Now look Lazarus, I have to give you the third degree, so my daughter won't accuse me of showing favoritism," Jerry said, escorting him into the living room. "Okay," Lazarus said, laughing. Jerry sat down with Lazarus and gave him a long stare. They busted out laughing. "Okay…Okay…on a serious note, Lazarus," Jerry said, looking serious. "It's true that you guys are adults, but my daughter is saving herself for marriage, if you know what I mean." Lazarus smiled at the fact that Ava was still a virgin. "Well, between you and me, Jerry, I'm still a virgin, too, and I plan on staying one until I'm married," Lazarus confessed. "Wow! Carl raised you right," Jerry said, smiling. Ava came downstairs wearing a beautiful dress. When Lazarus looked at her, he was mesmerized by her beauty. "Are you ready?" Ava said, smiling. "Yeah," Lazarus said, trying to focus. Jerry just snickered at poor Lazarus being so taken in with his daughter. "I'll see you later, Jerry," Lazarus said, shaking his hand. Lazarus escorted Ava out. She headed for her father's truck, but was shocked that Lazarus already had a blue mustang with him. "Lazarus, this is nice! Where did you get it?" Ava asked, looking at the nice car. "I got it from Mr. O'Brien for fixing his wine cellar," Lazarus said, opening the car door for Ava. Ava got in and waited for Lazarus. She noticed that Lazarus was wearing a nice shirt with some slacks, and wondered where they were going. Lazarus pulled up to a fancy restaurant called Judo's. "Lazarus, are you sure you want to come here? It's very expensive," Ava warned. "Yes, I'm sure," Lazarus said, opening the door and letting her out of the car. They went inside the restaurant and were seated by a waiter. "What can I start you off with?" the waiter asked. "What would you like, Ava?" Lazarus asked. "I'll take some of your red wine," Ava said to the waiter. The waiter then turned to Lazarus. "I'll have the same," Lazarus said, smiling at the waiter. Lazarus focused his attention on Ava. When Ava saw the look on his face, she knew he was pleased with how she looked. Soft music played in the restaurant. Occasionally, people would get up and start to dance. "I'm curious, Lazarus," Ava said, looking back at the couples on the dance floor. "About what?" Lazarus said, sitting back. "About how you found out that this was my favorite restaurant." "Let's just say I do my homework," Lazarus said, smiling. The waiter walked over with their wine. "Thank you," Lazarus said, nodding at the waiter. "Are you guys ready to order?" the waiter asked. "Yes, I will have the steak and the country potatoes," Lazarus said. "And you?" the waiter said, looking at Ava. "I'll have the same," Ava said, smiling. Lazarus stared at Ava as if he was mesmerized. "What?!" Ava said, feeling a little uncomfortable. "You are so beautiful," Lazarus said, sipping his wine. "I bet you say that to all the girls," Ava teased. "No, I don't," Lazarus said, in his defense. Ava laughed at Lazarus trying to defend himself; she thought he was adorable when he was on the defense. "Seriously though, you are the first woman that I have ever said that to," Lazarus admitted. "Well, I'm impressed!" Ava said, blushing. "So, tell me a little about yourself," Lazarus said, sipping his wine. "There's not much to tell. I'm a simple girl with a simple life. Most of the people in this town see me only as a preacher's daughter and that really irritates me." "Yeah, that would definitely irritate me, too," Lazarus admitted. The waiter came over with their meal. "Thank you," Lazarus said, as the waiter sat his plate down. "Thank you," Ava said as well. "This is so good!" Ava said, taking a bite of her steak. Lazarus just smiled. He took great pleasure in watching her enjoy herself. "What?" Ava asked, wondering what Lazarus was thinking about her. "Nothing, I just think it's cute how you are making a fuss over the steak, that's all." Embarrassed, Ava put her head down, trying not to blush. Lazarus lifted her head, staring deep into her eyes. He stroked her face as if he wanted to kiss her.

Julius sat across the room of Judo's restaurant with Marcus and his little brother, John. "So, what did Darla say about the Mr. Jordon file? Did she find it?" John asked. "No, she said it mysteriously disappeared," Julius said, while eating. "Man, that's too bad," John said, shaking his head. "What's up with you, Marcus?" Julius asked, punching him. "I was just wondering how things were with you and Ava," Marcus asked, staring at Ava and Lazarus at the other table. "I don't know, man. Ava's mad at me for walking out on her the other day," Julius confessed. "Is she seeing somebody?" Marcus asked. "What? Why are you so interested in Ava all of a sudden?" Julius asked. Marcus nodded his head, encouraging Julius to look across the room. When Julius saw the look on Marcus' face, he turned around and saw Ava and Lazarus having dinner together. Julius watched as Lazarus and Ava talked. He became extremely angry. "Maybe he's her friend or something," John suggested. "They don't look like friends to me," Julius snapped. "I know, dude. I've seen him around. Word is that he can fix anything," Marcus said. "Well, it looks to me he's trying to get with your girl," Marcus said, nodding at Ava and Lazarus.

Lazarus laughed at Ava as she picked through his plate. "I can't believe you're not full yet," Lazarus said, shaking his head. "Well, my Momma always says to never let food go to waste," Ava said, taking the last piece of meat from his plate. Lazarus sat back and stared at Ava. "Are you always this much fun, Ava?" "Well, I try to be," Ava said, smiling. Just then, some of the couples got up and started dancing. When Lazarus saw Ava staring at the couples, he figured that she wanted to get up and dance. "Would you like to dance?" Lazarus said, getting up. "Okay," Ava said, grabbing his hand. Lazarus led Ava to the dance floor. He pulled Ava up close to him and they started slow dancing. She looked deep into Lazarus' hazel eyes and felt as if she couldn't breathe. Lazarus knew that he had a certain spell over women, but when he saw Ava being taken in by his charm, he couldn't help but feel a little cocky. Lazarus wanted so badly for Ava to kiss him, but he just played it cool--trying to get her to make the first move. Ava couldn't take it any longer. She planted a soft kiss on Lazarus and then waited to see how he would respond. Lazarus grabbed the petite beauty up to him and kissed her passionately. The kiss was so heated that some of the other couples looked at them and smiled. "Ava!" a voice yelled, interrupting them. Ava looked up to see Julius standing there. "Julius!" Ava said, surprised. "What's this, Ava?" Julius said, looking at Lazarus. "Julius, this is Lazarus, and Lazarus, Julius." "Nice to meet you," Lazarus said, holding his hand out. Julius looked down at his hand and refused to shake it. "Can I talk to you for a minute, Ava?" Julius asked. Ava looked back at Lazarus and then at Julius. "Could you excuse us for a second, Lazarus?" Ava said. "Yeah, I'll be over at our table," Lazarus said, excusing himself. "What's going on, Ava?" Julius snapped. "Julius, keep your voice down, you're making a scene," Ava fussed. "I'm making a scene? I'm making a scene?! Ava, everyone in this town knows that we are going steady and you say that I'm making a scene?" "Julius, we can talk about this later," Ava said, trying to calm him down. "Well, that would be kind of difficult, being that you're not returning my calls," Julius snapped. "Julius, I'm not going to have this conversation here," Ava said, warning him. "Oh, I see. You're worried about your precious reputation. Daddy's little girl, right? Hate to disappoint daddy," Julius snapped. "You're a big jerk!" Ava said, walking away. Julius walked up behind her and grabbed her by the arm. "You listen here, Ava. I'm not one to let you or anyone else play me. I will make your life a living hell before I let that happen," Julius said, warning her. Ava became afraid. She had never seen Julius so mad. "Julius, let my arm go!" Ava demanded. "You heard the lady, let her go," Lazarus said, defending her. "Yeah? Who's going to make me?" Julius said, getting in Lazarus' face. Marcus and John ran over and grabbed Julius before anything got started. "Can we leave?" Ava said, looking at Lazarus with tears in her eyes. "Yeah," he said, escorting her to their table to get their things. Lazarus put money on the table to pay the bill, and then got Ava out of there as quickly as he could. Julius stood there, furious and embarrassed by Ava's behavior. "Come on, Julius, let's go to the bar and have a drink," John said, trying to calm him down. "Give us some scotch," John said. The bartender poured them their scotch. The bartender then looked at Marcus. "None for me, I'm the designated driver," Marcus said. "I can't believe this, man!" Julius said, taking a sip of his scotch. "I mean, how can Ava do this to me, man?" "Julius, you can have any girl in town. Quit tripping," John said, trying to comfort him. "I don't want any girl. I want Ava! And if this Lazarus thinks for one minute that he's going to come in and steal her, he better think again," Julius snapped. "Julius, just go home and get a good night's sleep. Give Ava time to cool off and call her," Marcus suggested. "Yeah, I'll call her. But in the meantime, John, I want you to find out everything you can about this Lazarus. Because when I'm done with him, he'll wish he was never born."

Chapter 5

Tears ran down Ava's face. She had never in her life been so embarrassed. Lazarus reached over and grabbed her hand, trying to comfort her. When they pulled up in the yard, Ava jumped out of the car before Lazarus could open the door for her. Lazarus turned the car off and darted up behind her.

Sissy sat on the sofa, looking out the window. "Sissy, what are you doing?" Marline said, walking into the living room. "Just watching Ava and Lazarus," Sissy admitted. "Sissy! That's eavesdropping!" Marline fussed. "You're right Mom, I'm sorry. I shouldn't be eavesdropping on Ava. Especially since it looks like her date didn't turn out too well." "What? Move out the way," Marline said, looking out the window. "Too easy," Sissy said, smiling.

Ava had a hard time looking Lazarus in the face. She thought for sure that Lazarus would think that she handled things irresponsibly. "Ava, look at me," Lazarus said, turning her around to face him. Ava looked up into his beautiful hazel eyes and began to cry again. "Lazarus, I'm sorry, I know what you must be thinking! I know that I should have ended things with Julius and..." Before she could say another word, Lazarus grabbed her and kissed her passionately. The kiss was so passionate that Marline covered Sissy's eyes. Lazarus continued kissing Ava. His strong hands gripped her tiny waist, and he pulled her closer to him. Once he let up, they stood there for a while, breathing heavily. "Can I see you tomorrow?" Lazarus said, sweeping his finger across her lips. "Yes," Ava said, gazing into his eyes. He planted a gentle kiss on her lips and walked away. Ava was blown away. She grabbed her keys out of her purse and headed for the front door. "Sissy, here she comes," Marline said, signaling Sissy to get out of the window. When Ava walked in, she closed the door behind her and exhaled. "Ava, is that you?" Marline asked, as if she didn't know. "Yeah, Mom, it's me," Ava said, coming in to join them. "So how was your date?" Marline asked. "Oh, Mom! It was perfect until Julius showed up. He almost ruined everything," Ava said, flopping down on the couch. "So, did this mess up things with you and Lazarus?" Sissy asked. "No, I'm going out with Lazarus again tomorrow," Ava said, smiling. "Does this mean you like Lazarus?" Marline asked. "What's not to like? He is so handsome, mom. I thought Julius was handsome, but Lazarus gives handsome a whole other meaning. He's also charming, and polite, and has this great sense of humor. Oh, Mom! I think I'm in love," Ava admitted. Marline touched her daughter's face. She was so happy that her daughter was finally experiencing happiness. "Mom, I've never met a man like Lazarus. He is so gentle and, to top it all off, he's a great kisser," Ava said, fanning herself. "Well, I'm happy you had a good time," Marline said, smiling at her daughter. Ava headed for the stairs. When she got half-way up the stairs, she turned around. "By the way, you guys forgot to close the curtains all the way," Ava said, shaking her head. Sissy and Marline looked at each other and started laughing at the fact that they were caught spying on Ava.

The next day, Ava awoke to the smell of turkey-bacon cooking. She smiled, thinking about the evening she'd spent with Lazarus. She got up and sat at her mirror, looking at herself. A knock on the door startled her. "Come in, Sissy," she said, as if she could see through the door. "How'd you know it was me?" Sissy asked. "Because you are the only person I know who knocks like a woodpecker. Anyway, what do you want?" "Well, I saw Lazarus this morning," Sissy began. "So?" Ava said, pretending not to care. "Oh, I'm sorry. I just thought you would want to know that he was over at Carmen's house." "Carmen's house! For what?" "Well, I think he was fixing something at her house, but you should have seen her flirting." "Why that little floozy!" Ava said, pouting. "It's okay, though. Lazarus paid no attention to her. It was like she didn't exist," Sissy said, laughing. "Really?" Ava said, smiling. "Yeah, really. I think his mind was on one woman, and that woman is you," Sissy said, winking at her sister, and leaving out.

Later that night, Ava waited patiently for Lazarus to show up. "How do I look?" Ava asked. "For the hundredth time, you look good," Sissy said, rolling her eyes. "Here he comes," Marline said, looking back and smiling at Ava. "Oh God," Ava said, trying to catch her breath. "Will you stop it! You don't want to seem desperate," Sissy said, shaking her head. "Okay you guys, get out of here," Ava said, fanning her mom and sister away. The doorbell rang. Ava opened the door and standing there, looking handsome as ever, was Lazarus. "Hey!" "Hey," Ava said, trying not to melt. "You ready to go?" he said, holding his hand out for hers. "Yes," Ava said, grabbing his hand. In the car, Ava watched Lazarus out of the corner of her eye, and when he would turn to look at her, she would turn away. Lazarus smiled at the fact that Ava was watching him. "You want to hear a little music?" Lazarus asked. "Sure," Ava said, blushing. Lazarus turned on the radio. "So, where are we going?" Ava asked. "It's a surprise," he said, smiling. Ava smiled too. She couldn't believe how handsome and down to earth he was. "Okay, I want you to close your eyes," Lazarus said, as he made a turn down one of the streets. Ava closed her eyes and waited with anticipation. "Keep them closed," he said, stopping the car. Ava smiled, because she could smell the water from the beach. "Okay, open your eyes." "Oh Lazarus, I love coming here," Ava said, putting her hands to her mouth. "Come on!" he said, pulling her arm. They set up a blanket on the grass near the beach. Ava sat there on the blanket with the wind blowing her long woolly hair. "This is just too much," she said, shaking her head. "I take it you're pleased?" "Yes, Lazarus! Thank you so much," she said, getting up and wrapping her arms around him. "You're welcome," he said, gazing into Ava's beautiful eyes. Ava wanted him to kiss her the way he kissed her the other night, but he just caressed her face and kept setting up. "What's this?" Ava said, grabbing one of the bowls that Lazarus had set down. "Oh, that's some soup. An old recipe my mom used to make." He opened a bottle of champagne and poured some in two glasses. He walked up to Ava and gave her one. Ava shivered when Lazarus walked up to her. "I want to make a toast," he said. Ava stared into his hazel eyes, mesmerized by his handsome face and his tall strong build. "To us, Ava, a new beginning," he said, hitting his glass with hers. "To us," Ava said, sipping her champagne. Again, Ava wanted Lazarus to kiss her, but he walked away. "Come on, before our food gets cold." They sat down and started eating the food that he had prepared. "This is really good," Ava said, while eating the soup. "Thank you," Lazarus said between bites. Ava had some of the soup dripping from her mouth and Lazarus seductively reached over, rubbed it off and licked his finger. Ava blushed and looked away. "So, Ms. Ava, what's up with you and this Julius guy?" "What do you mean?" "I mean, are you seeing him?" "I was, but it's just too complicated. Julius and I come from two different worlds. Julius was born into so much money, and I, on the other hand, was not. He thinks that I have commitment issues, but I just hate the way he sees life." "What do you mean?" "Well, for one, he talks badly about the poor. He's always putting them down and calling them lazy. I told him that's not true, and that I'm one of those people that he puts down, but he insists that it is true." "Man, that dude has issues," Lazarus said, shaking his head. "Tell me about it. He has this arrogance that makes him look down on others and I can't stand it. For instance, just now, when I had soup dripping from my face. That would have embarrassed him. He would never have done what you just did," Ava explained. "Well, no matter how he feels about the poor, he wants you. I can see it in his eyes," Lazarus admitted. Ava got quiet. "Do you see any future with this guy, Ava?" Lazarus asked. "No, Lazarus, I don't. I can't live this perfect life, where it's hard for me to breathe. I need someone that lets me be human and knows that I'm not perfect," Ava explained. Lazarus stared at Ava, and watched as she struggled with the whole conversation. "Hey," he said, touching her face, "It's okay. I'm here for you whenever you need me." Ava smiled and then turn away. "So, what about you, Lazarus?" "What about me?" "Have you ever had a special someone?" Ava asked. "No, I've always been the picky type, if you know what I mean." "Well, I'm sure you had a lot of girls trying to be with you?" "Yeah, but my father was real strict about me having girlfriends, and when I was old enough to have a relationship, I just found it hard because I stayed focused on my schooling." Ava got quiet. She loved the idea of not having some memory to compete with. "So," Lazarus said, breaking the silence, "I heard that you are a virgin." "What?! Who told you that?" "Calm down, your father made it perfectly clear that his daughter was a virgin and that he wanted it to stay that way." Ava shook her head, she was angry and embarrassed. "Hey," Lazarus said, grabbing her face, "there's no need to be upset. Besides, I'm a virgin, too." "You are?" Ava said, surprised. "Yeah, my father always stressed that if I wanted my wife to be a virgin, that I should be willing to be one, too." "Wow! Your father sounds like he was an extraordinary man." "Yes, he was," Lazarus said, smiling.

Chapter 6

Lazarus and Ava lay back on the picnic blanket and stared up at the stars. "What time does your father want you home?" "Excuse me, but I am a grown woman!" Ava said, getting sassy. "Really?" he said, throwing a piece of grape at her and hitting her in the head. "Why you little monster," Ava said, grabbing a piece of grape, hitting him back. "Oh, you want to play?" Lazarus said, throwing more food at her. Ava grabbed more food and started throwing food back. She grabbed a piece of bread and hit him in the head. "Hey! You're going to pay for that," Lazarus said, trying to grab her, but Ava jumped up and started running. Ava ran as fast as she could, but she was no match for Lazarus. He caught up with her and gently tackled her to the ground. He lay there on top of her, laughing and breathing heavily. Suddenly, their eyes met and a serious look crossed Lazarus' face. He leaned forward and started kissing her. The kiss started getting very passionate. Lazarus started rubbing her legs, and started going under her dress with his hands. "Wait, wait, wait," he said, pulling back. "What's wrong?" Ava said, trying to kiss him. "This isn't right," he said. "But I want too," Ava assured him. "Believe me, Ava, I would like nothing more than to take you right now and make love to you, but I promised your father that I would make sure that his daughter is brought back a virgin." "I understand. I guess we got carried away." "Yes, we did," Lazarus said, getting up. "Maybe we should call it a night," Lazarus said, reaching out his hand to pull her up. "Okay," Ava said, grabbing his hand. He pulled her up to him, and stroked her face. "Man, Ava, you just don't know what you do to me," he said, kissing her again. He then walked away from her and started gathering up their stuff.

The ride home was quiet, so Lazarus put on a tape and played slow songs. Every song that Lazarus played was like everything a girl would ever want to hear. Tears filled Ava's eyes because she was falling head over heels in love with Lazarus, and she was afraid of getting hurt.

When they pulled up to the house, it had started to pour down raining. "Great," Ava said, looking out at the pouring rain. "You want to make a run for it?" Lazarus said, smiling. "Yeah," Ava said, smiling back. "Ok, on the count of three." But before he could get to two, Ava dashed out into the rain and started running up to the house. Lazarus ran up behind her, trying to escape the rain. When they made it onto the porch, they started laughing. He grabbed Ava by her arms and started passionately kissing her. Ava pulled his tall masculine body to hers and wrapped her legs around his waist. "Lazarus, we better stop before I can't stop," she said, trying to catch her breath. "You're right. Maybe we should meet here at the house." "I think that's a good idea," Ava agreed. "Well, can I see you tomorrow?" Lazarus asked. "You can see me whenever you want," Ava assured him. He then leaned forward and kissed her goodnight.

The next day, Ava was lying on the couch reading a magazine when the doorbell rang. "Sissy!" Ava yelled, not taking her eyes off of the magazine. "What?!" Sissy said, out of breath from running down the stairs. "Answer the door," Ava demanded. "Are you kidding? You are right here, Ava!" Sissy complained. "Yeah, but I'm reading," Ava argued. Sissy rolled her eyes and stomped all the way to the front door to answer it. When she opened the door, Lily and Sandy were on the other side. "Hey, Sissy!" they both said. "Whatever!" Sissy said, walking away. Lily and Sandy ignored Sissy's rude behavior and let themselves in. "Ava, what's up girl?" Lily said. "Hey you guys," Ava said, surprised to see her two friends standing there. "So, where have you been, missy?" Sandy said, slapping Ava's leg. "With Lazarus," Ava said, blushing. "Oh snap!" Sandy said, fanning. "Girl, it's better you than me, because if it was me, I would have about five kids already," Lily said, teasing. "So, Ava, what's he like?" Sandy asked. "Oh Sandy," Ava said, shaking her head, "He is so polite and so charming." "Why come she always finds the good ones?" Lily said, rolling her eyes. "So, give up details, did you kiss him?" Sandy asked. "Yes, over and over and over again," Ava bragged. Sandy and Lily busted out laughing. "I'll tell you something else, too," Ava said, motioning her friends to come to her bedroom. When they got inside the bedroom, Ava closed the door and they all flopped on the bed. "What is it?" Lily asked in anticipation. "We almost did it," Ava confessed. "Did what?" Lily asked. "You know…it." "What?!" Lily said, looking at Sandy, surprised. "I know you're lying to me, Miss I'm Waiting Until I'm Married," Sandy mocked. "I know, it's weird, because all I can think about when I'm with him is sex," Ava confessed. "Well, I can understand that," Sandy said, clapping Lily's hand. "So, when are you going to see him again?" Sandy asked. "Tonight," Ava said. "Man, this sounds serious," Lily said. "Yeah, sounds to me, Ava, like you're falling in love," Sandy agreed. "I am," Ava said, getting serious. Lily looked at Sandy and then at Ava. "What about Julius?" Lily asked. "It's over," Ava said, looking away. "What do you mean it's over?" Lily asked. "We have grown apart, that's all, and besides, I'm falling in love with Lazarus." "Julius isn't going to like this, Ava," Lily warned. "Yeah, he's been asking about you, wondering if we have seen you. He said you're not answering his calls," Sandy said. "I know. I don't know what to do. I told Julius I wasn't ready for a commitment, but he refuses to let go," Ava explained. "Well, I hope everything works out with this Lazarus, because you are giving up a lot with Julius," Lily said. "And why is that, Lily? Because he has money?" Ava snapped. "Not only that, he's good-looking, smart, and he has a lot going for himself, Ava," Lily fussed. "Well, so does Lazarus!" Ava snapped. She then went over and stared out of the window. Lily looked at Sandy, wondering if they had said too much. "Ava, we didn't mean any harm," Lily began. "Yeah Ava, we just want you to be happy, that's all," Sandy agreed. "I know you guys mean well, and you don't want me to make a mistake, but when I'm around Lazarus, I feel so complete. He has this hold on me that I can't explain. I'm in love with him and I'm so afraid," Ava confessed. Sandy and Lily grabbed Ava and gave her a hug.

Months later, Ava was helping to set the table for dinner, when the doorbell rang. She knew it was Lazarus. "Hey Sissy, can you open the door for Lazarus?" Ava asked. "Sure, and only because it is Lazarus," Sissy snapped. Ava rolled her eyes and kept setting the table. "Hi Lazarus," Sissy said, when she opened the door. "Why hi, Miss Sissy," Lazarus said, pinching her cheek. "What's that?" Sissy said, pointing to a gift in his hand. "Why this is for you," he said, giving her the gift. "Oh, thank you, Lazarus!" Sissy said, running through the house with her gift. "Hi Lazarus," Marline said. "Hey Marline," Lazarus said, giving her a hug. "These are for you," he said, giving her a bouquet of flowers. "Thank you, Lazarus, this was so thoughtful," Marline said, smelling the flowers. He then looked over at Ava and was speechless. Marline saw the way he looked at her daughter. "I'll just go and put these in some water," Marline said, and she left, giving them some privacy. Lazarus walked over to Ava and hugged her. He held her as if he was never going to see her again. Ava had no desire to let him go, either. She looked into his eyes and kissed him. "Well, well, well, it looks like love to me!" Jerry said, walking in. "Dad!" Ava said, looking embarrassed. "Hey Jerry," Lazarus said, shaking his hand. "Hey Lazarus." Ava decided to give the men some privacy. She gave Lazarus a seductive smile and left to help her mom in the kitchen.

Later, the girls came in with the food and they all sat around the table. Jerry opened up with prayer, thanking God for each other and their food. At first, everyone was quiet and just ate their food. Ava sat patiently, watching Lazarus chow down. Ava then gave her mother a certain look. "Okay, what is going on?" Jerry said, busting the two of them out. "What?" Marline said, trying to look innocent. "I see the two of you watching Lazarus and giving each other signals with your eyes." "Oh Jerry, shut up and eat your food!" Marline fussed. "No. Not until someone explains to me what's going on." "Okay," Marline said, looking at Ava like she had no other choice. "It is tradition in my family that if a man loves your meatloaf, that man will love you for forever. And, well, when Ava saw how Lazarus chowed down on her meatloaf, we just got excited. That's all." "Really? I didn't like your meatloaf, Marline," Jerry confessed. "What?!" Marline said, looking surprised. "I'm just kidding," Jerry said, laughing. "So, let me get this straight. Me liking Ava's meatloaf is a sign that I will love her for forever?" Lazarus asked. "Yes," Marline said. "In that case..." Lazarus started chowing down on the meatloaf like there was no tomorrow. Ava and everyone at the table busted out laughing at Lazarus. Ava then gave him a warm smile in the midst of everybody's laughter.

After dinner, Lazarus and Ava walked out on the porch, holding hands. "Dinner was great. Thank you for everything," he said, gazing into her eyes. "I'm glad you liked it," Ava said, smiling. "No, I loved it!" Lazarus said, teasing. Ava hit him for teasing her. "It's still kind of early. You want to catch a movie?" Lazarus asked. "Sure, I'll just let my parents know," Ava said, going inside to tell her parents that she was leaving.

Chapter 7

Lazarus and Ava sat at the movies, watching a comedy. Ava could barely get her popcorn down, she was laughing so hard. Lazarus just sat back and watched her. He took great pleasure in seeing her so happy. Ava stopped laughing when she noticed him staring at her. "What?" she asked. "Nothing," he said, caressing her face. He pulled her up to him and kissed her. Ava was so engaged in their kiss, but Lazarus had to pull away. "Hey, I'm sorry," Lazarus whispered. "Sorry for what?" "Sorry, because this is definitely not honoring God." Ava put her head down. "You're right, why don't we just call it a night?" Ava suggested. "Yeah, I think we better," Lazarus said, grabbing her hand and leading her out of the movies.

When they got to Ava's house, Lazarus escorted her to the door. "Well, I had a good time tonight," Ava said, trying not to look him in the face. "So did I," he said, lifting her face up to meet his. He started to kiss her, but Ava turn away. Lazarus realized that was his cue to leave, so he just kissed her on the forehead and left. Tears filled Ava's eyes, as she watched Lazarus drive off down the road. She was definitely in love with him.

The next day, Ava sat at the window, staring outside. "He's at Mr. Thomas's house," Sissy said, coming in. "Who?" Ava said, pretending that she had no clue about what Sissy was talking about. "Lazarus!" Sissy said. "That is who you're thinking about, isn't it?" "Sissy, get out of my room!" Ava snapped. "Hey…I come in peace. Why are you so

30

grumpy?" Sissy fussed. "I'm sorry, Sissy. I am a little on edge," Ava admitted. "Let me guess…you have fallen madly in love with Lazarus, but you are afraid that he may not feel the same, and if you tell him how you feel, you could very well jeopardize your relationship." "How on earth did you know that?" Ava asked. "Oh, I watched 'Love Coast' last night," Sissy admitted. "Sissy, why are you watching romantic movies?" Ava asked, shaking her head. "Because I'm trying to learn the language of love," Sissy said, smiling. "You are too much," Ava said, shaking her head. "So, what happened in the movie? Did she tell the guy how she felt?" Ava asked. "Yes," Sissy assured her. "And?" Ava asked with anticipation. "Well, after she told him, she got hit by a train and died," Sissy said. "What?!" Ava said, in disbelief. "I'm just kidding, Ava. She told him how she felt and they lived happily ever after." "Well, it's too bad that real stories never end up like those in the movies," Ava said, looking out of the window. "Well, I think I hear Mom calling me," Sissy said, rolling her eyes. Ava threw her arm up, letting Sissy know it was fine. Sissy shook her head at her sister. Ava's mood was really starting to irritate her. Sissy let herself out of Ava's room and raced down the stairs as fast as she could. "Where are you going, young lady?" Marline called behind her. "I'll be right back, Mom! I have a mission from God," she said, as she hopped off the porch onto her bike. "Was that our daughter just flying through here?" Jerry asked. "Yes, and I'm afraid of what she's up to," Marline admitted.

Lazarus stood on the sidewalk in front of Mr. Thomas' house, fixing his fence. He was just about to dig another hole when Sissy interrupted him. "Hey, Lazarus," Sissy said, riding up, out of breath. "Well, well, well, what a lovely surprise," Lazarus said, putting his shovel down and squatting down in front of her. Sissy blushed at the handsome smile that he flashed her. "So, what brings you by?" Lazarus asked. "Well, I have something I need to discuss with you," Sissy said. "Oh, what's that?" Lazarus asked. "How do you feel about my sister?" Sissy asked. "I beg your pardon?" Lazarus said, confused. "How do you feel about, Ava?" Sissy asked. "I don't think I understand. Why you are asking me about my feelings towards your sister?" Lazarus said, looking at her curiously. "Okay, you pulled it out of me. Ava is driving me nuts with her attitude these days. And it's all because she's madly in love with you and she's afraid that you don't feel the same about her." "How do you know she's in love with me?" Lazarus asked. "She said it!" Sissy blabbed. Lazarus started smiling. "Hey! Let's get one thing straight. You didn't hear this from me," Sissy said. "Yeah, I know," Lazarus said, nodding his head. "So?!" "So what?" Lazarus asked. "So, what are you going to do about this mess?" Sissy fussed. "I'll tell you what I'm going to do," he said, getting up and walking over to his car. He pulled something out of the glove compartment and brought it over to Sissy. When he opened the tiny box, Sissy's eyes got big. "Is that…" "Yes, it's an engagement ring for Ava," Lazarus said, interrupting her. "Wow!" Sissy said, in disbelief. "Hey! Don't tell anyone that you saw this," Lazarus said, putting the ring away. "I won't," Sissy assured him. "So, when are you going to ask her?" "I don't know, but after talking to you, I feel a little lucky tonight," Lazarus said, smiling.

Later that night, Sissy waited with anticipation for Lazarus to arrive. "Sissy, I notice you've been staring out that window all day. Who are you looking for?" Ava asked. "Oh, I was just looking for Lazarus," Sissy said, staring out the window again. "Why? You don't normally look for Lazarus," Ava said, giving her a 'you're up to something' look. "I just wanted to see him that's all. He's a lot of fun," Sissy explained. Ava sat down next to her sister and put her arm around her. "You really like him, huh?" Ava said, smiling. "Yeah, he's a cool guy," Sissy said. Ava took a deep breath and started stroking her sister's long hair. "Hey! What are you doing? You need to be upstairs getting ready. You don't want Lazarus to see you looking like that," Sissy fussed. Ava gave her sister a shove. "You are really good for my self-esteem," Ava said sarcastically. She then got up to go freshen up. Sissy was about to get up when the doorbell rang. She hurried over and opened the front door, and there on the other side was Lazarus. "Hey! What took you so long?" Sissy said, pulling him in the house. "I wanted to make sure that I was looking good. Tonight is an important night," Lazarus admitted. "You look fine, Lazarus," Sissy assured him. "So, where is everybody?" Lazarus said, looking around. "Well, my dad is in his office, mom is in the kitchen, and your bride-to-be is upstairs, putting on her face,"

Sissy explained. Lazarus shook his head at her and headed to Jerry's office. When he got to the door, he took a deep breath and knocked on the door. "Come in," Jerry said, without knowing who was at the door. When he looked up and saw Lazarus, he was surprised. "Lazarus, hey! Is everything alright?" Jerry asked. "Yes, I just wanted to talk to you for a minute, if you've got the time?" Lazarus said. "Sure, sit down Lazarus," Jerry said, motioning him towards a chair. Lazarus made his way over to the chair and sat down. "So, what is it you want to talk about?" Jerry asked. "I won't beat around the bush, Jerry. I'm in love with your daughter," Lazarus blurted out. "Well, that's no surprise to me, a blind man could see the connection between you two," Jerry said, laughing. Lazarus smiled nervously as he watched his friend laugh. "Wait a minute, you two haven't..." "No!" Lazarus said, cutting him off. "I have too much respect for you to do something like that." "Well, now I am curious," Jerry said. "I want to ask Ava to marry me tonight and I want your blessing," Lazarus said. Jerry got up and stared at him for a long time, and then broke out into joyful laughter. They started hugging. "What's going on?" Marline said, coming in. "Lazarus is going to ask Ava to marry him," Jerry said. "What?! That's great!" Marline said, hugging him. "Well, you get out there, I don't want her to catch you talking to us," Jerry said, shoving him out. Lazarus walked out and took a deep breath. He then sat with Sissy while she was deep into a movie on television. When Ava finally came downstairs, she took his breath away. "Hey!" he said, giving her a nervous smile. "Hello, Lazarus," Ava said, gazing into his beautiful eyes. Lazarus looked as if he wanted to kiss her, so Ava walked away as quickly as she could. "So...I was thinking that maybe we can watch a movie or something tonight," Ava said, giving Sissy a look to get lost. Sissy rolled her eyes and left. Lazarus could feel distance between himself and Ava. He walked over to her and gently grabbed her arm. "I was thinking that we could just go somewhere, where we can be alone, and talk," he suggested. "We can go out on the porch if you like." "Okay," Lazarus said, leading the way. Ava could feel her heart sink. "What if he wants to break up?" she thought. She tried hard not to let her insecurities show. They both sat there quietly, rocking back and forth on the porch swing. "Ava, what's going on?" Lazarus said, breaking the silence. "What do you mean?" Ava said, not sure what he was talking about. "I mean, what is this between us, this distance?" Ava got up and walked to the edge of the porch. Lazarus took a deep breath and followed her. "How do you feel about me?" he asked, as he gently turned her around to face him. Ava looked at his handsome face. She had never in her whole life been afraid of anything the way she was afraid of the hold he had on her. She tried to walk away from him, but he grabbed her up to him. "Ava, what is this? Do you not want to be with me anymore?" Lazarus demanded to know. "No," Ava said, wiping away tears that were streaming down her face. "Then what's going on? Why can't you tell me what it is you're feeling?" "I'm just confused, that's all," Ava admitted. "Confused about what?" "I don't know, I guess about this relationship," Ava said. "What's confusing you?" Lazarus said, stroking her face. Ava couldn't answer him, and she couldn't stop the tears that were pouring down her face. "Do you love me?" he asked, wiping the tears from her eyes. Ava felt her heart sink. "What?" Ava said, surprised. "Do you love me, Ava?" "Lazarus, I'm not sure." "Ava! Forget the games! Do you love me?" he demanded. Ava could see the frustration in his eyes, and she knew that he would not let her go until she admitted the truth to him. "Yes!" she blurted out. Ava's heart raced when Lazarus walked away from her. She was wondering if it was a mistake to admit her feelings. The expression on his face made her nervous. "Lazarus, please say something. If you don't feel the same way, I understand. I'm not pressuring you to love me back," Ava assured him. "Does this tell you how I feel?" He got down on one knee and pulled a diamond ring out of his pocket. Ava put her hands over her mouth in shock. "Ava, will you marry me? Will you make me the happiest man in the world?" Lazarus asked. "Yes, yes, yes!" Ava blurted out. He then got up and picked her up, spinning her around. When Marline heard the commotion outside, she knew that Ava had said yes. "Hey, I think she said yes," Marline said, motioning Jerry to the window. Lazarus put Ava down and put the ring on her finger. "It's a perfect fit," he said, smiling. "It's beautiful," Ava said, admiring it. "It belonged to my mother." Ava looked at him and smiled. Lazarus pulled his bride to be up to him and started kissing her. When they saw the porch lights blinking on and off, they started laughing and went inside to tell the family the good news. When they walked inside, Ava had no doubt in her mind that they already knew. "Well, from the look on your face, Lazarus, I take it she said yes," Jerry asked. "Yes, she did, she agreed to be the future Mrs. Sanford," Lazarus said, hugging her. "Congratulations!" Marline and Jerry shouted. "So when are you guys planning on getting married?" Marline asked in anticipation. Lazarus looked at Ava, putting the ball in her court. "Well, I was hoping the sooner the better," Ava said, looking into Lazarus eyes, trying to make sure that was okay with him. "Any day is fine with me. I'd marry you today if I could," Lazarus said, stroking her cheek. Ava smiled at him and threw her arms around him, hugging him as tightly as she could. "I'm so happy and I love you so much," she assured him. They started kissing passionately. "Excuse me, but you two aren't married yet," Jerry said, interrupting them. "Sorry, Daddy," Ava said, embarrassed. "So what about this weekend?" Lazarus asked. "It will be my 23rd birthday and that would be the best birthday gift in the world." Ava gazed into his beautiful hazel eyes for a moment. "Daddy, can you marry us this weekend?" Ava said, not taking her eyes off of Lazarus. "I can definitely do that," Jerry said, hugging Marline. "Well, it's settled then. We will get married this weekend!" Ava said, smiling at her future husband.

Chapter 8

Ava lie on the bed, staring at her beautiful diamond ring. The idea of becoming Lazarus' wife was so surreal to her. A knock on the door soon took her out of her fantasy land. "It's me," Sissy said, letting herself in. "Come on in, sis," Ava said, smiling. "Wow! You really are in love," Sissy said, shaking her head. "Now, why do you say that?" Ava asked. "Because you're being nice to me, that's why," Sissy said, flopping down on the bed. "Well, I have to be nice to my maid of honor," Ava said, rubbing Sissy's head. "Are you serious? You want me to be your maid of honor?" Sissy asked. "Yes, I do. If it weren't for you, I wouldn't be getting married tomorrow," Ava said. "Wow! I don't know what to say," Sissy said, getting up. "Well, I hope you say yes." "Of course! I mean, yes!" Sissy said, with excitement. Ava walked over to her sister and gave her a long hug. "Thank you so much, Sissy," she said, with tears in her eyes.

The next day, Lily, Violet, and Sandy sat in the dining room, confused about why they had to be there early in the morning. "What is this all about?" Violet asked. "I wish I knew. All I know is she told me it was vital that I be here and to dress up," Sandy said. "She told me the same thing," Lily argued. "Well, I want to know what on God's green earth is going on," Violet said, getting up to confront Ava. Just then, Ava came out. "Finally!" Violet said. "Yeah, what is going on, Ava?!" Sandy argued. "Girls, calm down," Ava said, motioning them to sit down. "So?" Lily said, in anticipation. "I'm getting married today,"

Ava confessed. "What! To who?" Violet asked. "Lazarus," Ava answered. "What!?" Lily said, in disbelief. "Congratulations!" they all said. "Man, I was just telling myself this morning that it better be a good reason why you got me up out of my beauty sleep," Violet said. "Well, is this good enough?" Ava asked. "Yes," Violet said, with tears in her eyes. "Well, I can see why you couldn't tell us what was going on. You couldn't risk Julius finding out," Lily said. "Lily, now is not the time," Violet argued. "No, I'm just saying I understand. I mean, if Julius would have found out somehow, he probably would have stopped the wedding," Lily explained. "She's right, I couldn't risk Julius finding out. And please, if you all don't mind, don't tell anyone about this until I've had a chance to tell Julius," Ava explained. "Okay," they all agreed. "Well, we better get to the church," Ava said.

Ava and the girls arrived at the church around 9 o'clock. When she made it in without running into Lazarus, she let out a big sigh. Sissy came in, already dressed in a beautiful white dress. "Aw, Sissy, you look adorable," Sandy said, hugging her. "Yeah Sissy, you clean up pretty good," Lily said. "She sure does," Violet agreed. "Thanks, you guys," Sissy said, blushing. "Well, did you see Lazarus?" Ava asked. "Yes! And believe me when I say he looks so good," Sissy said. When she said that, they all got excited about seeing Lazarus in a tuxedo. "Girl, I bet you can't wait for the honeymoon," Lily blurted out. "Lily, you are terrible," Ava said, hitting her. "Yeah, plus Sissy's ears are too young for that kind of talk," Sandy agreed. "Oh, grow up, Sandy," Sissy said, in disgust. They all started laughing when Sissy said that.

The wedding started at noon. Lily, Violet, and Sandy all took their seats. Lily notice the familiar decorations, that she saw at previous weddings. Only a few attended the wedding. One was a high school friend who flew in to be Lazarus' best man, and two of Ava's aunts. Lazarus stood at the altar talking to Jerry. Lazarus seemed to be really nervous, but he kept his cool. When Marline came out smiling, everybody knew that it was time. Lazarus got into position and took a deep breath. Just then, Sissy and his high school friend, Terry, came down the aisle. Lazarus smiled when he saw how beautiful Sissy looked. After they took their position, the organ player started playing the wedding tune, "Here Comes the Bride." When Ava stepped out, she took Lazarus' breath away. She was absolutely breathtaking. She wore a long white gown that showed off her tiny waist. Her hair was pulled back into an elegant style and she wore her makeup very light. Marline smiled at her daughter as she made her way down the aisle, knowing that all of her hard work in making her daughter's wedding dress paid off when she saw how beautiful Ava looked in it. Lazarus was mesmerized. Everyone else in the room seemed to disappear when he saw Ava. When Ava made it up to the alter, he grabbed her hand and kissed it. "Let us all pray," Jerry began. "Heavenly Father, we come together to join together these two souls in marriage. I pray that you would give us your blessing, and bless Lazarus and Ava with a prosperous future. In Jesus' name, amen."

Lazarus and Ava exchanged their vows. Jerry announced them husband and wife. "Lazarus, you may now kiss your bride." Lazarus pulled Ava up to him and they started kissing. They laughed as the cheers went forward.

At the reception, everyone was gathered around Ava and Lazarus, taking pictures and congratulating them. Next, they had a nice dinner. Lazarus all of a sudden started eating out of Ava's plate. When Ava saw her husband eating out of her plate, she hit his hand. They both started laughing. When people saw the moment between them, they rang their bells for them to kiss. "Well, you heard the people," Lazarus said. He grabbed her gently and they started kissing. "Hey, save all that for the honeymoon!" his friend Terry joked.

After dinner, they played music and it was time for the husband and wife to dance. Ava's face lit up when she recognized the song that Lazarus chose. It was the song that he played in the car on the night of one of their dates. He pulled her close and they started slow dancing. Lazarus started singing some of the song into her ear and she was blown away. "I didn't know you could sing," Ava said. "I can't, not really," Lazarus said, grazing his finger across her mouth. Ava got chills through her body every time he did that. "So, where are we going after we leave here?" Ava asked. "It's a surprise," Lazarus admitted. Ava stared at her husband, wondering what he was up to. She then decided to let it go.

"Did you pack a bag like I asked you to?" Lazarus asked. "Yes, I did," Ava said. "Okay, your only job right now is to be ready for whatever I have planned." "You're not going to give me a hint?" "No!" Lazarus said, kissing her on the forehead and ending the dance with that. They then had the father and daughter dance, and Lazarus escorted his wife over to his new father in-law. Jerry gave Lazarus a hug when he brought Ava over. When Jerry wrapped his arms around Ava, she immediately fell into his arms and wept. "It's okay, baby," he said, holding his daughter. It dawned on him how needy she was for his love. "Hey, you are going to ruin your makeup," he said, rubbing the tears away from her eyes. Ava tried to wipe away her tears, but as quickly as she wiped them away, more came pouring down. "I want you to know something. You are still my girl, and if you ever need me, I'm here," he said, looking into her eyes. Ava grabbed him and they hugged for a long time. Marline watched the two and could not hold back her tears. Lazarus then grabbed her hand. "May I have this dance?" he said. "Yes, you may, but I have to warn you, I'm the queen on the dance floor." Lazarus laughed and escorted his mother-in-law to the dance floor. They started to dance. After their dance, they had cake. Ava was worried that Lazarus would try to smash the cake in her face, but he gently put it in her mouth and ended it with a kiss. The guests all cheered. When Ava was done with the cake, her girls whispered something in her ear. "Okay!" Ava agreed. They turn on some music and started to dance. It was one of the dances they did in school, when they were cheerleaders. The guests all cheered and Lazarus was blown away by his wife's moves. After the dance, Lazarus gave her a nod, letting her know that he was ready. He couldn't wait any longer to have her in his arms. "Oh, I know that look," Lily teased. "Well, we are going to get going," Ava said. She started saying goodbye to everybody. "Hey Terry, you remember what we talked about?" Lazarus whispered. "Lazarus, everything will be fine. Just let it flow naturally," Terry assured him. "This will be my first time and I don't want to ruin it," Lazarus worried. "You won't, trust me man, the first is always a little scary, but you two have the rest of your lives to get it right. Besides, with a hot little number like Ava, I think it will be easy to figure it out." "Yeah, I guess you're right. I'm up," he said, clapping his hand and giving him a hug. Lazarus escorted Ava to the car. "Did you put your suitcase in the trunk like I asked?" "Yes, honey!" Ava said, getting in the car. They waved at everybody one last time and drove away. On their way to the airport, Lazarus was quiet. Ava was curious as to what he was thinking. All of a sudden, he pulled the car off the road. Ava was shocked by Lazarus' behavior and she wondered what he was doing. "Lazarus, what's wrong?" Ava asked. He just stared at her for a minute. "I want you," he began. "What! Now?" Ava asked, confused. "Yes, I mean, I was hoping that we could just go to a hotel." "But we have a flight, don't we?" "Yeah, but we really don't have to leave until tomorrow." Ava got quiet. She was nervous, and of course she wanted Lazarus as bad as he wanted her, but she was a little worried about pleasing him. "Hey, I have waited my whole life for you, so please excuse me if I come off a little desperate," Lazarus said. "I love you, and if you want to go to a hotel, I want that too," Ava said, touching his face. He took off towards a nearby hotel.

"May I help you?" the clerk said from behind the front desk. "I need a room. A suite if you have one." "Yes sir, we do. They run three hundred a night. Is that okay?" "Yes, we will take it," Lazarus said. He gave her a credit card and she got his keys for him.

Ava could feel her heart pounding as they made their way to their suite. "Wow!" she said, looking around the room. "You like it?" Lazarus said, closing the door behind them. "Yes! It's so big and elegant," Ava said, looking around. "Well, you deserve it," he said, touching her face. Ava looked up at him. He looked so handsome in his tuxedo. "I can't believe you're mine," Ava said, staring into his eyes. Lazarus said nothing. He just grabbed her up to him and started kissing her passionately. He picked her up and took her to the bedroom. He gently lay her on the bed and started to take her dress off. "Wait!" Ava yelled. "What's wrong?" "Nothing, I just want to slip on the lingerie that I bought." "You sure that's all?" "Yes," Ava said, getting up and stepping into the next room to get her bag. She went in the bathroom and let out a big sigh. Lazarus turned on a radio that was in the room and turned the dial to some soft music. Ava could hear the music playing and got nervous. "Get a hold of yourself, Ava," she said to herself. She took her long hair out of the bun she was wearing and let it all hang down. She then put on her gown. "Okay, I can do this," she said, looking in the mirror. A knock on the door startled her. "Ava, are coming out?" "I'll be right there," she said, taking a deep breath. "Do you not want to do this?" Lazarus asked. "Yes, I just need a minute, that's all," Ava said, burying her face in her hands. Lazarus started getting tired of waiting, so he went over and got in the bed. When Ava finally came out, her appearance wiped away his frustration. Lazarus sat up in the bed, unable to take his eyes off of her. "Well, what do you think?" Ava asked nervously. "You are so beautiful," he said, getting up. He walked over to her and stroked her long hair. "Are you ready?" he asked gently. "Yes!" Ava said, looking into his loving eyes. He led her over to the bed. Lazarus began kissing and caressing her. Ava could feel every part of her body longing to be touched by him. When he finally started making love to her, she could feel the pain of making love for the first time. Ava gripped his back in pain. When Lazarus looked down at her, he saw tears in her eyes. "Am I hurting you?" he asked. "It's fine," Ava said, wiping a tear from her eye. "Do you want me to stop?" "No," Ava said. "Are you sure?" Lazarus asked. Ava said nothing. She just started kissing him, letting him know that it was alright and they continued making love.

The next morning, Ava woke up to the smell of coffee. She got up and put on Lazarus' shirt, which was on the floor next to the bed. When she walked into the dining room, she spotted Lazarus sitting at the table reading a newspaper. "Good morning," he said, kissing her. "Good morning," Ava said, sitting down at the table. "Did you sleep okay?" "Yes, I slept like a rock," Ava said, smiling. "Well, I ordered room service." "I see," Ava said, grabbing a plate. She started fixing herself a plate. "Looks like you ordered the whole kitchen," she said jokingly. "Yeah, I wasn't sure what you wanted," Lazarus admitted. "So, what time are we leaving?" Ava asked, while chewing on some bacon. "I was thinking about 3 o'clock." "Why so late?" Ava asked, confused. "Because it will give me a chance to make love to my beautiful wife again," he said, pulling her on his lap. "You are so bad," Ava said, kissing him.

Later that day, Ava and Lazarus boarded the plane. During their flight, they mostly slept. Lazarus woke up to the announcement that the plane was about to land. "Baby, wake up. We are here," Lazarus said, shaking her. "We are?" Ava said, stretching. "Yes, come on," Lazarus said, grabbing her hand. When they made it out of the airport, a taxi cab took them to their hotel. "I can't believe we are in California!" Ava said, smiling. "Believe it baby!" "Can we afford this?" Ava asked. "Yes, my father had a little something put away for me before he died," Lazarus confessed. Ava stared out of the window, looking at all the beautiful palm trees. "It's so beautiful here," Ava said. Lazarus looked at his wife's excited face and laughed. When they got out of the cab, Lazarus paid the cab driver and checked into the hotel. When they got into their hotel room, Ava dropped her bags and ran straight to the balcony. "Oh Lazarus, I love it," Ava said, looking around. "So, what do you want to do?" Lazarus asked. "I want to go sight-seeing, but first I need a shower," Ava said, rubbing her finger through her tangled hair. "Why don't I give you a real reason to get showered," Lazarus said, rubbing his finger across her lips. He knew when he did that, it made Ava crazy. Ava looked at him for a second and then raced him to the hotel's bedroom.

Chapter 9

Jerry sat on the couch watching a football game. He was interrupted by a knock on the door. When he went over to answer the door, standing on the other side was Julius. "Julius!" Jerry said, surprised. "May I come in?" "Sure. Where are my manners?" Jerry said, stepping aside and letting him in. Julius came in, looking around the house as if he were looking for something. He smelled of alcohol and looked as if he had lost his best-friend. "Is Ava here?" he said, not beating around the bush. "No Julius," Jerry admitted. "So, it's true, isn't it? Ava married Lazarus?" When he asked that, Jerry was shocked. "How did you find out?" Jerry asked. "I figured it out the other day when I saw Violet dressed up with a bouquet of flowers," Julius admitted. "Julius, I'm sorry, I don't know what to say," Jerry said, putting his hand on his shoulder. "It's not your fault Jerry. I mean… you can't make your daughter love me," Julius said, with hurt in his eyes. "Is there something I can do for you? Can I pray with you?" Jerry asked. "No! I just need to be alone right now." "I'm really sorry, Julius," Jerry said. Julius said nothing, he just left the house.

Lazarus and Ava were lying in front of the fireplace with just a blanket around their naked bodies. She rubbed his arm, which was wrapped around her tiny waist. "Ava, are you sleep?" Lazarus asked. "No," Ava said, turning around to face him. "Are you alright?" Lazarus asked. "Yes, making love to you is the best feeling in the world," Ava said, stroking his face. "That's not what I mean," he said, grabbing her hand and kissing it. Ava tried to turn away from him, but he gently turned her face back to his. "What's got your mind," he asked, "or shall I ask who?" Ava could feel her heart racing. "Baby, you know that I only want you," Ava said. "I know, but you have been thinking about Julius, haven't you?" Ava was speechless because it was true. "Hey! I understand, you want to tell Julius about us." When Lazarus said that, Ava was relieved. "Yes, I do. I know that I handled this whole thing wrong. I should have told him about my feelings for you in the beginning. Lazarus, I have to be the one to tell him, before someone else does," Ava said, hoping that her husband would understand. "You have my support if you want to tell him," Lazarus said. Ava then wrapped herself in his arms.

A few days later, they made it home. Lazarus pulled up to the house that was once his, but now belonged to him and his wife. When Ava saw the house, she was shocked. The once abandoned house was painted and had beautiful landscaping. "Lazarus, when did you do all of this?" Ava asked in amazement. "From day one," he said, pulling the suitcases out of the car. "Wait till you see the inside," he said, putting the suitcases on the porch and picking her up. Ava was turned on by her husband's strength. He opened the door and walked into a neatly furnished house. "Wow!" Ava said, looking around, "This place looks great!" "I'm glad you like it," Lazarus said, putting her down. "Where did you get all of this?" "Well, I bought a lot of it from thrift shops." "This stuff looks brand new," Ava said, feeling the wood on the tables. "Well, once I got it, I refurbished it." "Well, I'm impressed," Ava said, shaking her head. "Would you like to see the bedroom?" Lazarus asked. "Sure," Ava said, wondering if he was up to something. When Ava went into the bedroom, her eyes lit up. "Lazarus, this is great," she said, looking around. Lazarus watched as she looked around the bedroom and the master bathroom. "You remodeled the bathroom!" "Yeah," Lazarus said, laughing at her reaction.

Later that night, Ava was on the phone talking to her mom. "Where is Daddy?" "He had a meeting at the church," Marline said. "Why didn't you go with him?" "Well, because I was a little tired," she admitted. "So, how are things going with you and my handsome son-in-law?" "It's great, Momma. I am so happy. Lazarus fixed up the house. Did you see it yet?" "Yes, I did. He is really talented." "Well Mom, I better get off this phone. I'm trying to fix our first meal and I don't want it to be a disaster," Ava said, stirring the food on the stove. "Okay baby, I will talk to you later." "I love you, Mom." "I love you, too," Marline said, hanging up the phone. "How is it going?" Lazarus said, hugging her from behind. "It's going good," she said, taking a spoon of her pasta to give him a bite. "Ummm… that's good." "Good," Ava said, turning the stove off. Lazarus went over and started setting the dining room table. "Who was that on the phone?" "It was Mom," Ava said, putting the rolls and pasta on the table. Lazarus opened a bottle of wine and poured it into their glasses. He also lit a few candles. "Well, this looks romantic," Ava said, smiling at her husband. "Yes, it does." He then grabbed Ava's hand. "Shall we pray?" he said, bowing his head. "Heavenly Father, we thank you for this meal and each other. Please bless our food, for the nourishment of our bodies. In Jesus' name, amen." They started digging in. "I have to get back to work tomorrow," Lazarus said, breaking the silence. "Already?" Ava said, disappointed. "Yes, I have to be able to provide for my beautiful wife, don't I?" "Yeah, I guess," Ava said, pouting. Ava looked at Lazarus, wondering if it was the right time to talk about Julius. She took a deep breath and decided that she would. "I was hoping to see Julius tomorrow," she began. "Oh?" Lazarus said, pretending not to care. "Yes. Are you okay with that?" Ava said, sipping her wine. "Yes, I trust you," he said, getting up and leaving out. When Lazarus left the table, she realized that it was a bad time to bring up Julius. She got up, blew out the candles, and followed him into the room. "Hey!" Ava said, turning him around. "I didn't mean to upset you. I just want to do the right thing, that's all. I don't like hurting others and I feel that's what I've done to Julius," Ava explained. "Look Ava, I know I said I was okay with this whole thing, but I just got a bad feeling about this," Lazarus admitted. "Lazarus! Nothing will go wrong. It's you I love. I just want to tell him before someone else does," Ava explained. "I guess I'm being a little insecure," Lazarus said, touching her face. "You don't have to be, because I'm yours. Forever." "Have I told you how much I love you?" He said, rubbing his finger across her lips.

"No! Why don't you show me?" Ava flirted. "With pleasure!" he said, picking her up and laying her on the bed. They started making love.

After they were done making love, Ava lay in her husband's arms. "I never knew that letting go felt so good," Ava said, rubbing his chest. "I know," Lazarus said, kissing her on the forehead. "Lazarus, I know we haven't discussed it yet, but one day I hope to give you lots of babies." "Oh really! Would you like to get started right now?" he said, flirting. "No! We just did it!" she said, hitting him. Lazarus laughed at his wife getting so worked up. "Hey, I have something for you," Lazarus said, reaching over and getting a small box off of the nightstand. "What is it?" Ava said, sitting up. "It's something I picked up in California," he said, handing it to her. Ava opened the box and it was a beautiful necklace. "It's beautiful!" she said, with tears in her eyes. She turned around so he could put it on her. "Thank you!" she said, kissing him. She drifted off to sleep, wrapped in his arms.

The next morning, Ava woke up and there was no sign of Lazarus. "Lazarus!" she yelled, but there was no answer. She saw a note on the nightstand that said:

> *Hello, my beautiful wife. I didn't want to wake you, because you were sleeping so peacefully. I went to work and I will see you later tonight.*
>
> Love, Lazarus

Ava smiled at the note that Lazarus had left. She got up and showered. After her shower, she carefully played in her mind, over and over, what she would say to Julius. She put on a beautiful sundress and decided to wear her hair down. She felt that she still wanted to look her best, even if it would be her last time seeing him.

When Ava arrived at Julius' house, she took a deep breath and knocked on the door. When the door opened, there on the other side was Julius' maid, Mary. "Hi Mary! Is Julius home?" Ava asked nervously. "Yes! Come in," Mary said cheerfully. Ava waited patiently while Mary went to get Julius. "He can see you now," Mary said, motioning for her to go into his office. When Ava walked into his office, he had his back to her, staring out the window. Ava closed the door behind her and walk over to him. "Julius, it's me, Ava," Ava said. "I know. I can smell your perfume. I always liked that perfume. What's it called?" "Julius, we need to talk," Ava said, ignoring his comment. He turned around to face her. "Well, don't you look beautiful today." "Thank you," Ava said, looking away. "So, what is it you want to talk about? Do you want to talk about how you stomped all over my heart, Ava, or maybe you want to talk about your marriage to Lazarus?" Julius snapped. "You know," Ava said, putting her hand over her mouth. "How could you do it, Ava!?" he yelled. Ava jumped. She had never seen him so upset. "I never meant to hurt you." "You never meant to hurt me. Well, you did! I was willing to give you everything I have. Anything you ever dreamed. Why, Ava, why did you do this?" he said, grabbing her by the arms and shaking her. "I'm sorry Julius, I'm so sorry," Ava said, crying. "You're not sorry. From the moment he came, you have treated me like an outcast." "Please Julius, forgive me," Ava pleaded. Julius glared at her for a moment. "If you want me to forgive you, you will get this marriage annulled." "I can't do that, I love him," Ava confessed. "You don't even know him, Ava!" Julius snapped. "What is it Ava? What does he have that I don't, huh?" He grabbed her and slammed her up against the wall. "What is it Ava?" he said, grabbing her face. Ava tried to get away, but he was too strong. Julius pinned her to the wall. "What are you doing? Please stop!" Ava yelled. Ava finally got away from his strong grip and tried to run, but he caught her before she could get away. "You have disrespected and betrayed me in front of all my friends and family," he said, grabbing her by the arm. "Please Julius, you're hurting me," she said, trying to get away from him. "I'm hurting you? What about me, Ava? All this time I've wasted on you. And for what, Ava?" he shouted. "Let me go!" Ava yelled. She tried to push him away. When she did that, it angered him and he slapped her. Ava held her face in disbelief and started swinging at him, but she was no match for him. She hit him in the face and he smacked her with the back of his hand. Ava fell to the ground, gasping for air. The blow to her face knocked the energy out of her. She tried getting up, but she stumbled and fell down again. Just then, John came in. When he saw Ava on the floor, with blood on her mouth, he gave his brother a serious glare. John went over to Ava and picked her up off the floor. "Are you alright?" he said, wiping her tears with his hand. Ava nodded her head, but then burst into tears. John held her in his arms and looked at his brother as if he wanted to strangle him. "Do you need me to take you home?" John asked. "No, I'm okay," Ava said, trying to convince him that she was strong enough to make it home by herself. "Okay. Get out of here, Ava. Go home to your husband," John said, rubbing her arm. Ava nodded her head and looked back at Julius, who was still very upset. She saw herself out. "What were you thinking? You hit women now?" John snapped. "Calm down," Julius said, watching Ava out the window. She made it to her car and broke down crying again. "Julius, this isn't like you, hitting a woman. I thought you still loved her," John said, shaking his head. "I do," Julius said, going over to his bar to pour himself a drink. "Julius, she married another man. You have to learn to live with that." "No!" Julius shouted. "Ava belongs with me and there is no way I'm going to lose her to some loser like Lazarus." "Julius, don't you get it? You already have lost her," John said, yanking him around. "John, she means everything to me," Julius said, drinking his bourbon. "Julius, I know you love her, but it's time to let her go," John said, grabbing his shoulder. Julius ignored his comment and kept drinking his bourbon. "I plan to get her back," Julius admitted. "Plan to get her back? Are you hearing yourself? The woman is married, Julius." "She won't be for long," Julius said, with confidence. "What on God's earth are you planning?" "My revenge!" Julius said. "Julius, you are scaring me, man." "John, you know me, if I want something, I get it," Julius argued. "Well, do you honestly think you're going to get a woman like Ava by hitting her? Whatever you're plotting, Julius, you better let it go before it blows up in your face. Are you even thinking about her husband's reaction when he sees her face? He is going to want to come over here and kill you!" John argued. "I'm banking on that, John. It's all part of my plan," Julius said, with a mysterious look on his face.

Ava sat at the kitchen table, sobbing. "Mom, how does it look? Do you think Lazarus will be able to tell?" Ava asked. "Ava, we have had ice on your face for most of the day and it still hasn't gone down. Sweetheart, there is no way you can hide this from your husband. Your eye is practically closed," Marline argued. "Maybe I can tell him that I slipped in the shower." "Ava, you don't want to start off a marriage lying," Marline said, holding her daughter's face in her hands. "Oh Momma! What have I done?" Ava said, crying. Marline held her daughter in her arms and comforted her. Just then, they heard the door open. "Oh God! It's Lazarus," Ava said, trying to adjust herself. "Well, I better get going so you two can talk," Marline said.

Marline met Lazarus as she was leaving. "Hey Mom," Lazarus said, kissing her. "Hey Lazarus," Marline said, rubbing his arm. "You're leaving?" "Yes, I have to get home to help Sissy with homework," she explained. "Okay," he said, letting her out. Lazarus came into the kitchen and grabbed Ava from behind. "Hey, my beautiful wife, I have been thinking about you all day," Lazarus said, kissing her on the neck. "I've been thinking about you, too," Ava said, walking away so he wouldn't see her face. She walked over to the sink and started to wash the vegetables. Lazarus could sense that she was avoiding him, that something was wrong. "Ava, is everything alright?" Lazarus asked. "Yes honey, I'm just tired, that's all," Ava lied. "Well, turn around and talk to me," Lazarus said, rubbing her back. Ava turned around to face her husband. She looked up at him and he couldn't believe his eyes. "Ava, what happened?" Lazarus said, grabbing her by her arms. "Ah!" Ava said, screaming from Lazarus' touch. Lazarus looked at her in shock. He pulled up her sleeve and saw bruises on her arm. "Who did this?" he demanded to know. "It's okay honey, I will be alright," Ava said, trying to convince him. "Who did it, Ava?!" Lazarus yelled. "He was just upset, that's all," Ava said, trying to reason with him. "Did Julius do this?" Ava said nothing, she just put her head down. That let Lazarus know that it was Julius. He grabbed his keys off of the table and stormed out of the kitchen. "Lazarus, please don't go over there," Ava begged. But she couldn't convince him. He jumped in his car and sped off.

Julius stood around, talking to some of the guests at a party that he put together at the last minute. "What are you up to?" John said, walking up. "You will know soon," Julius said, sipping his wine. Just then, they heard a loud knock on the door. "He is right on time," Julius said, smiling. "Who is?" John said, confused. Mary walked over to the door and opened it, and before she could say anything, Lazarus stormed past her. He walked up to Julius and hit him in the face. Guests stared in disbelief at Lazarus. "Don't ever put your hands on my wife!" Lazarus yelled, "As a matter of fact, you stay away from her!" "Lazarus, you seem upset," Julius said, wiping the blood from his mouth. "Why you…" "Lazarus, you need to go," John said, grabbing him before he could take another shot at his brother. "You touch her again I'll kill you," Lazarus said, yanking his arm away from John and walking out. When he finally made it home, Ava ran to the door. "Lazarus, are you alright?" Ava said, grabbing him when he came in the door. "Yeah," he said, holding his hand. Ava looked down at his hand and knew that he had been in a fight. "What happened, Lazarus?" Ava said, grabbing his hand. "I'm okay," he said, grabbing a bowl from the kitchen and filling it with ice, so he could stick his fist in it to relieve the swelling. "So, what happened, Ava?" Lazarus asked. "Well, I went over there to tell him that I was married, but he already knew. I told him that I was sorry for hurting him, but he was too angry to understand. He went into this rage because I said that I loved you, and he started grabbing me and hitting me," Ava said, with tears in her eyes. Lazarus was furious at the story that Ava had just told. "I should have kept hitting him," he said, hitting the table. Ava nervously jumped and put her hands to her mouth when Lazarus hit the table. When Lazarus saw how upset she was, he grabbed her hand from her face. "I'm sorry Ava, I didn't mean to scare you," he said, pulling her over to him. "I would never hurt you," he said, holding her. He gently touched her face, but every time he looked at her eye and mouth, he was tempted to go back and confront Julius. "I must look horrible," Ava said, putting her head down. "Hey," he said, lifting her face up, "you are still beautiful." Lazarus kissed her. "Well, I have your dinner in the fridge. Do you want me to warm it up?" "No, I'm not really hungry," Lazarus said, "Come on, let's go and get some rest," he said, hitting her on the butt.

Ava lie in her husband's arms. She felt so safe when his strong arms were wrapped around her. "Are you mad at me?" Ava asked. "No! Why do you think that?" Lazarus said, stroking her hair. "Because I went, even when you felt uneasy about the situation." "Baby, I know you meant well," he said, kissing her on the head. "How did I get so lucky?" Ava said, looking up at him. She started kissing him. Lazarus kissed her gently, because of her cut lip. "Make love to me," Ava said, rubbing his chest. He flipped her over and got on top of her, and started making love to his wife. Later that night, as they slept, someone banged on the door and woke them up. "Who could that be?" Ava said, looking at Lazarus. Lazarus got up and slipped on his pants. Ava just wrapped a sheet around her naked body. When Lazarus opened the door, there on the other side was the police. "May I help you?" he said, looking confused. "Are you Lazarus Sanford?" the police asked. "Yes," Lazarus said. Ava came out to see who was at the door. When she saw the police, she had an uneasy feeling in the pit of her stomach. "You are under arrest," the policeman said, taking his handcuffs out and turning Lazarus around to cuff him. "For what?!" Lazarus demanded to know. "For breaking and entering and armed robbery," the police explained. "Officer, there must be some mistake," Lazarus tried to explain. "There is no mistake, Mr. Sanford. We have eye witnesses." "Officer, I assure you, you have the wrong man," Ava pleaded. "Sorry ma'am, just doing my job," he said, taking him out to the car. Ava broke down in tears. "Ava, call and get me a lawyer," Lazarus said, as he was being shoved into the police car. Ava stared in disbelief as the police drove out of sight. When she was about to go inside, something caught her eye. It was Julius, standing across the street, leaning against his limousine. He lit a cigarette and walked across the street to greet her. Ava could feel her chest beating out of control. When he came up to her, she dashed inside and tried to close the door, but he grabbed it and held it with his strength. Julius inhaled his cigarette, dropped it on the floor and put it out with his shoe. "Get out!" Ava shouted. "Baby, is that any way to greet your future husband?" Julius said, smiling. "You wish," Ava snapped, "You did this, didn't you?" "Ava, I'm hurt that you would even suggest such a thing." "You won't get away with this, Julius," Ava snapped. "Oh, I believe I will. As a matter of fact, before this is over, you will come to me, begging me to let up on that little trophy husband of yours." "Julius, please! You are mad at me. I'm the one who hurt you, not Lazarus. Please, punish me," Ava pleaded with him. Julius was tempted. He saw that she was wearing nothing but a sheet. He walked closer to her and she gasped. He was just as much of a temptation for her as she was for him. He gently grabbed her by the arms. Ava froze with fear. "I still want you Ava, and you will be mine," he said, trying to kiss her, but Ava turned her head. "I could never be with you, Julius," she said, with hate in her eyes. "I know that you are mad at me right now, but in the end, you will know that I'm doing this for us." He stroked her face and then left. Ava locked the door and fell to the floor crying.

Days later, Ava and Jerry sat in the court, waiting for Lazarus' trial. When Lazarus came in, Ava stood up. Jerry grabbed his daughter to restrain her. "He'll be alright, baby," he whispered. Julius came in with an attorney. When he saw Lazarus, he winked at him. Finally, the judge came in and everyone in the court stood up. The trial was short and simple. The judge heard both sides and asked for Julius and another eye witness to testify against Lazarus. When the judge gave Lazarus a bail of one million to get out, and a sentence of 10 years, Ava broke down into tears. The guard put the handcuffs back on Lazarus and escorted him out. Jerry held Ava in his arms while she sobbed.

Later that day, Ava stared helplessly out of the window. She had cried until she was exhausted. "Can I get you something to eat?" Marline asked. "No, Mom," Ava said, looking out of the window. "Honey, you have to eat something," Marline argued. "I will, later," Ava assured her. "Ava, I'm worried about you. You have been at that window for most of the day, crying." "Mom, my husband's in jail," Ava snapped. "I know honey, and I'm sorry that there is nothing we can do," Marline said, with tears in her eyes. "There is something I can do," Ava said, getting up. "Where are you going?" Marline asked. "I'm going to fix this problem," Ava said, leaving the house. She went home and took a shower. After that, she found a seductive dress to put on. She wore her hair down and put on some makeup. She then made her way to Julius' house.

Chapter 10

Ava arrived at Julius' house and knocked on the door. When the door opened, she expected it to be Mary, but it was Julius. "May I come in?" Ava asked. Julius looked her up and down, and was well pleased with her appearance. He stepped aside to let her in. "What can I do for you?" he asked, walking over to the bar and pouring himself a drink. "You know why I'm here, Julius" Ava snapped. Julius looked at her, confused. "So, where do you want to do it?" Ava asked. "Do what?" Julius asked. "Don't play games with me, Julius!" Ava yelled. "I get it. You want to see me beg." She walked over to him and started kissing him on the neck and rubbing on his chest. "Ava, my darling, as flattering as this is, and I do mean flattering, I don't want to have sex with you. At least, not now. No, the deal is, I will get Lazarus out of jail if you get the marriage annulled and marry me." "What!?" Ava said, looking at him in disbelief. "You heard me, and there is no use talking me out of it because I won't bend." "There is no way that I'm leaving my husband, Julius," Ava snapped. "Well, I guess I underestimated your love for Lazarus. I didn't think you would let the man you love rot in prison," Julius said, drinking his scotch. "You're sick if you think that you can blackmail me into marrying you," Ava snapped. "Okay, it's your call," he said, taking another sip of his drink. Ava scoffed at him and rolled her eyes as she stormed out, slamming the door behind her. "That was brilliant," a voice said from behind. It was John. He took his brother's drink out of his hand and drank some of his scotch. "Do you think she'll bend?" John asked. "Well, that all depends on her love for him," Julius said. "Why didn't you just have her tonight?" "Because I want all of her," Julius explained. "Well it must have been hard turning her down." "You have no idea," Julius said, shaking his head. "So, what's the plan now?" John asked. "It's time to make this a little more real for her. She needs to know that Lazarus is not away on a business trip, but with hardcore criminals," Julius said, with a devious smile. The next day, Ava waited patiently to see Lazarus. When he finally came out, she was in disbelief. He had a black eye and some bruises on his face. "Lazarus, what happened?" Ava cried. "It's nothing baby, just some guys trying to test me," he said, trying not to worry her. Ava was lost for words, she just started sobbing. "Hey, you have to be strong. God will get me out of here somehow." "How Lazarus!? How are we going to come up with all that money!?" Ava snapped. "We have to have faith and wait on God," Lazarus explained. "Well, I don't have the faith that you have right now," Ava snapped. "Baby please! I need for you to be strong," Lazarus said. "Okay," Ava said, nodding her head.

Later that night, Ava was on the couch watching TV, trying to keep her mind off of Lazarus. A knock on the door startled her. She got up and opened the door. There, on the other side, was Julius. Ava let him in and closed the door. "If you've come here to try to get me to take your offer, you're wasting your time," Ava snapped. "Well I must say that I'm surprised. I thought that seeing Lazarus beat up, you would bend," Julius said. Ava looked at him in shock. "You set that up, didn't you?" Ava asked. "Yes, I did, and if you do not cooperate, your little Lazarus will become somebody's girl." "How could you do this?" Ava asked. "I don't want to, Ava, so don't make me," he said. "I will be expecting an answer tomorrow. I already have the divorce papers drawn up. So you decide tonight. Lazarus' safety or his destruction." He got ready to leave, but stopped and turned around. "Don't play me, Ava. I'm a well-respected man in this town, and I can make Lazarus' life a living hell," Julius said, as he walked out.

The next day, Ava sat at the prison waiting for Lazarus. When he came out she took a deep breath. "Hey baby," he said, picking up the phone. "Hi," Ava said, putting her head down. "I talked to my lawyer today and he said that he thinks that he can get me out." "Lazarus, I'm getting our marriage annulled!" Ava blurted out. "What did you say?" "You heard me, Lazarus, I'm signing the divorce papers when I leave here, and I will be marrying Julius." "What do you mean, you're marrying Julius? Why are you doing this?" "Lazarus, please! It's the only way to get you out of here," Ava explained. "Ava! I would rather rot in here than to lose you," Lazarus snapped. "I'm sorry Lazarus, it has to be this way. Besides, Julius could make your life a living hell in here." "You think I care about that? Julius don't scare me! Ava, we serve a God that is way more powerful than Julius." "I'm sorry, Lazarus," Ava said, getting up. "Ava!" Lazarus said, yelling at the glass. "Don't do this," he said, hitting the glass. "Please forgive me," Ava said, crying. "Ava! Ava! Ava!" Lazarus screamed. He was so upset that a guard had to grab him and restrain him.

Later that night, Ava arrived at Julius' mansion around 7 o'clock. When he opened the door, she was standing there with her suitcases in her hands. Tears streamed down her checks and no matter how hard she tried, she could not stop them. He grabbed her arm and pulled her into the house. He took her suitcases out of her hands and pulled her up to him and held her in his arms. "I know you don't see it right now Ava, but I love you, and there is no way that I can live without you." "Where's the papers?" she asked, wiping the tears from her face. "Right here," he said, motioning her towards the table. Ava stared at the document as if she wanted to change her mind, but she grabbed the pen off of the table and signed it. She buried her face in her hands and started crying. "I will make you happy Ava, I promise," Julius said, holding her in his arms.

Weeks later, Ava stayed in bed until noon. Julius knocked on the door and let himself in. "How long are you going to lie around, Ava?" he asked. Ava said nothing, she just lie there. "Ava, we have a wedding to plan," Julius said. "How can I forget?" Ava said, getting up. "Hey," Julius said, grabbing her arm. "I hope you don't think you're going to do this half-hearted. I have some important people coming tonight and if you embarrass me in anyway, I promise you...you will be sorry." "I'm not going to embarrass you in front of your precious friends and family," Ava said, rolling her eyes. "I want this attitude of yours to stop. And another thing, Lazarus will not make bail until we have consecrated our marriage," he said, lifting her face up to his, making sure that they had an understanding. Ava looked at him and knew that he meant every word. "Get yourself together. A lady will be here shortly with some wedding dresses for you to pick out," he said, leaving. Ava took a bubble bath in the beautiful Jacuzzi tub that was connected to the guest room. Shortly after she got dressed, there was a knock on the door. When she opened the door, an older lady carrying loads of wedding dresses was there on the other side. "Ava?" "Yes," Ava said. "Good, do you mind?" the lady said, handing some of the dresses to Ava. Ava grabbed the dresses and put them on the bed. "I'm Betty," she said, reaching her hand out. "Nice to meet you," Ava said, shaking her hand. "You know, your fiancé was right about you." "Yeah, about what?" Ava asked. "He said you were breathtaking," Betty said. Ava tried hard not to blush. "Let me look at you, you're about a size 6 right?" "Yes, that's right," Ava said. "Okay, I think I know the perfect dress that will bring your type of beauty out." She pulled out a long, elegant white gown. The gown took Ava's breath away. "Wow, this is beautiful," Ava said, holding it up to herself and looking in the mirror. "It looks so expensive," Ava said, rubbing the fabric. "Well, it is," Betty admitted, "this dress is $356,000." "Wow, this costs more than anything I've ever owned." "Would you like to try it on?" Betty asked. "Sure," Ava said, slipping her robe off and sliding the dress on. "Don't you look lovely," Betty said, adjusting the train on the dress. Ava stared at herself in the mirror. "It seems like Julius wants the best for me," Ava said, admiring herself in the mirror. "I'll say," Betty said, pulling out a box. "What's that?" Ava asked. "It's a little something that your fiancé wants you to wear." Ava opened the black box and she was blown away. In the black box was a diamond necklace, diamond earrings, and a diamond tiara. "Wow! Is this real?" Ava said, looking amazed. "Yes! This set is one million dollars," Betty said, gently taking the necklace out of the case. Betty put the necklace on Ava. When Ava looked at herself in the mirror, tears filled her eyes. "He must really love you," Betty said, smiling at her in the mirror. "Tell me something Betty. Is it wrong to be in love with two men?" Ava asked. "Well, that sounds complicated. I will say this, if you are having doubts, now is the time to confront those doubts, because after you say 'I do' today, that's it. But I will say this, you don't find too many men that would go through all this trouble to make his woman happy," Betty assured her. Ava gave Betty a forced smile.

Later that night, Ava was all set. She sat on the bed talking to her mom on the phone. She was already made up and had her hair pinned up with her million-dollar tiara, diamond necklace and earrings. "Mom, please understand, I have to do this. It's the only way Lazarus will be safe," Ava argued. "I understand that you want to keep Lazarus out of danger Ava, but don't expect your father and I to support a man who is blackmailing you. I know this is destroying you, and I just can't fix myself to watch. Now, I talked to Jerry and he feels the same. He's hoping that you will come to your senses and trust God." "I am trusting God, Momma. I'm trusting God not to condemn me for what I am about to do," Ava said. Betty came in. "It's almost time. We have to get you into your dress," Betty said, pointing to her watch. "Momma, I have to go," Ava said, looking at Betty. "Okay honey, I love you and will be praying for you," Marline said. "I love you, too," Ava said, hanging up the phone. Ava put her head down. "Are you alright?" Betty said, sitting down beside her. "Yes," Ava said, fighting back the tears. "Well, everyone is in place, and I have to get you out there in five minutes," Betty said, grabbing her dress. Ava slipped on her dress and when she turned around, Betty got emotional. "You will take his breath away," Betty said, smiling.

Ava stood at the doors to the dining area. When they opened the doors for her, she was amazed at how beautiful it looked. Julius had beautiful flowers everywhere. When guests saw her, they all stood up to honor her. They looked with amazement at how beautiful she looked. Julius smiled. He was completely blown away. When she made it up to him, he grabbed her hand. "You look beautiful," he said, kissing her. "Julius, we are not at that part yet," the minister said, laughing. "Hey Rev. Can you skip all the long stuff and just get to it?" Julius whispered. "Okay," the minister said. "Ladies and Gents. We come before you to unite Julius Willingham and Ava Benjamin. Julius, will you take Ava to be your lawfully wedded wife?" "I do," Julius said, gazing into her eyes. "Ava, will you take Julius to be your husband?" Ava thought about Lazarus, what it would do to him. She then looked into Julius eyes and for the first time she saw how vulnerable and insecure he was. Julius took a deep breath because Ava was taking too long to answer. The crowd started talking amongst themselves. Ava saw the look of embarrassment on Julius' face. "I'm sorry," Ava said, "I just got a little nervous marrying such a powerful guy," she said, to save him from embarrassment. Julius and everyone in the place started to laugh. When the crowd got silent, Ava answered. "I do." "You may now kiss your bride," the minister said, smiling. Julius grabbed Ava up to him and kissed her passionately. The guests all cheered and some of the photographers took pictures. After the exchange of the vows, they all celebrated. Ava was standing with a bunch of Julius' friends, being admired for her beauty. Julius watched his new wife impress the crowed. "So, you pulled it off," John said, patting him on the shoulders. "Yeah, I did," Julius said, smiling. "So are you really going to get Lazarus out of prison?" "John, you know I'm a man of my word. Besides, if I don't, Ava will never forgive me." "So, how are you going to keep her away from him?" John asked. "Don't worry, I got it all planned out," Julius said, sipping his wine. "Hey Julius, you lucky dog!" Marcus said, hugging him. "How in the world did you get Ava to finally commit?" Marcus asked. "Believe me, it wasn't easy," Julius confessed. "I don't understand. Wasn't she married to Lazarus?" Marcus asked, confused. "Hey! Keep it down! Not too many people know that," Julius whispered. "So, what happened with that?" Marcus asked. "Marcus, I will tell you later," Julius said. "I bet you can't wait for the honeymoon," John said, looking at Ava and shaking his head. "Come on John, you know I'm ready," he said, clapping his hand. "You are one lucky man," Marcus said, sipping his wine. "Yes I know," Julius said, looking at his wife.

Later that night, Ava sat in the master bathroom, freshening up for bed. Julius was lying in their bed, patiently waiting for her. He had candles lit and rose pedals all over the floor and bed. When Ava came out, he was mesmerized. She walked over to the bed and sat down next to him. "Are you alright? You're shaking," he said, rubbing her arms. "Julius, do you love me? Or is this all a game to you?" Ava asked. "Ava, you know I love you," he said, caressing her face. "I don't think I can do this, Julius," she said, crying. "Ava, you are my wife now and there is nothing wrong with you giving yourself to me," Julius said, grabbing her face. "Don't deny me Ava, not now," he said, kissing her. When he saw that she didn't pull away, he kept kissing her. Julius took his shirt off and he was so masculine and handsome. At that moment, Ava realized that she was in love with him, too. He lay her on the bed, and before they knew it, they were making love.

Julius woke up around 2 o'clock in the morning. When he looked over and saw that Ava was gone, he got up, slipped on his pants, and started looking for her. He heard noises coming from the kitchen and so he turned on the lights. "I'm sorry! Was I loud?" Ava said, while digging in the refrigerator. "Ava! It's two in the morning!" Julius fussed. "I'm sorry, I got hungry," she admitted. "Come sit down," Julius said, grabbing her hand. "Let me cook for you," he said. "What do you want?" "Just a sandwich," Ava said, grabbing an apple out of a bowl that was sitting on the counter. "I didn't know you cooked," Ava teased. "There is a lot you don't know about me," he said, kissing her on the forehead. "Julius, why didn't you make me sign a prenuptial agreement?" Ava asked. "Because whatever I have is yours, Ava," he said, handing her the sandwich. At that moment, Ava realized how much he truly did love her. "This is good," Ava said, taking a bite. Ava quickly ate her sandwich. When she finished, they went upstairs and got in bed. Ava lie there in bed thinking about her relationship with Lazarus. She was totally in love with him, but she couldn't deny what she was feeling for Julius. "Julius, are you awake?" Ava asked. "Yeah," he said, turning around in the bed to face her. "I just want to thank you for such a lovely wedding," Ava began. "You don't have to thank me, Ava," Julius said, rubbing her arm. "I know under the circumstances, you could have done things differently," Ava said. "Ava, I love you. I've always loved you, from the moment we first met," he said. "Julius, will you make love to me again?" she asked. He looked at her, surprised. "Are you sure?" "Yes," Ava said. They started kissing passionately and then started making love.

The next day, Ava stayed in bed until noon. After she got showered, she went downstairs to find Julius. "Hi Mary, have you seen Julius?"

Ava asked. "Oh, he told me to tell you that he went to bail Lazarus out," Mary said. Ava was very happy, but nervous at the same time. "Would you like me to fix you something to eat?" Mary asked, interrupting her thoughts. "Sure, Mary," Ava said, smiling. But her smile soon faded away when she thought about Lazarus finding out about her marriage to Julius.

Julius sat patiently, waiting for Lazarus to show up. When Lazarus finally showed up, he scoffed angrily at Julius sitting there. "What do you want?" Lazarus asked, when he picked up the phone. "Is that any way to talk to the person who is about to get you out of jail?" Julius mocked. "Why should I be thankful? You are the one who put me here in the first place!" Lazarus snapped. "Lazarus, calm down," Julius said, smiling. "I come in peace. Besides, my wife would be really upset if she knew we weren't getting along." "If you're talking about Ava, she would never marry you," Lazarus snapped. "Oh, but she did. As a matter of fact, we made the front page," Julius said, holding up a newspaper to the window that separated them. Lazarus' heart sank when he saw a picture of Ava and Julius kissing. "Doesn't she make a beautiful bride?" Julius mocked. "You think that picture means something?" Lazarus said, pretending not to care. "We both know that you blackmailed her to marry you. Ava will never love you, Julius." "I don't know, Lazarus. I felt the love last night, over and over again," he said, smiling. "You're dreaming," Lazarus said, angrily. "No, I'm not. Ava committed herself to me last night in every way. As a matter of fact, she screamed my name, not yours. You know something, I like the birthmark that she has that sits right between her…" "Shut up! Shut your filthy mouth!" Lazarus shouted. "You are making all of this up. Ava would never do this to me. She loves me!" Lazarus screamed. Julius sat back and watched Lazarus break down, enjoying every moment. The guard ran over and grabbed Lazarus' arms. "Lazarus, if you don't control yourself I'm going to have to take you back," the officer said. Tears ran down his face and he looked at Julius as if he wanted to kill him. The officer finally calmed Lazarus down and he sat back at the booth. "Why are you doing this?" Lazarus asked. "Because I hate you, Lazarus. You came into this town, acting like you were above everybody, and go after my girl. To put it simply, you made war with me when you went after Ava. And now that she's my wife, I want you to stay away from her, or I'll make your life hell," Julius said, getting up. "Who do you think you are? You're just mad because it's me she loves!" Lazarus yelled. "You hear me, Julius? It's me she loves!" He kept yelling, but Julius ignored him and walked out.

Chapter 11

A va sat at the window, waiting for Julius to come home. When she saw the limo pull up, she ran to the front door to greet him. "Hey," Julius said, walking in. "Hi," Ava said, hugging him. Julius went over to the bar and poured himself some sparkling water. "I guess you're wanting to know if I got Lazarus out of jail?" he said, taking a sip of his water. "Well, did you?" Ava asked, trying not to sound anxious. "Yes! He should be on his way home as we speak," Julius said, drinking the rest of his water. "Thank you, Julius," Ava said, hugging him. "Well, I always keep my promises," Julius admitted. A knock on the door startled them. Julius went over to answer the door and there on the other side was John. "You're just in time," Julius said, clapping his hand. "Hi Ava," John said, when he spotted the beauty standing there. "Hi John," Ava said, waving. Ava looked at John with his briefcase. "Should I leave you two to your work?" she asked. "I'm sorry, baby, John and I have a lot of paper work to get done," Julius apologized. "I understand. I was going to ask you anyway if I could pick up a few things at the store," Ava said. "Sure," Julius said, giving her one of his credit cards. "Get whatever you want," he said, kissing her. Ava looked into his eyes, feeling guilt. She then waved goodbye to John and left. John walked over to the sofa and set his briefcase down. "So, married man, how was the honeymoon? Was it worth the wait?" John asked, while pulling some of his papers out of his briefcase. "Yes John, it was definitely worth the wait," Julius said, laughing. "You lucky dog," John said, shaking his head. "I have to admit, I didn't think Ava would go all the way." "Well she did, and she wanted more," Julius bragged. "What!? You're kidding!" John said, looking surprised. "Believe me, I was shocked myself, but there she was, asking me to make love to her again." "So, do you think your wife will go and see Lazarus?" John asked. "Yeah. As a matter of fact, I'd put all my money on the fact that she went to see him right now," Julius said, pulling more papers out of John's briefcase. "Okay, that doesn't bother you that she's probably going to see him?" John asked, confused. "No, it's all part of my plan," Julius said, getting up and pouring himself a drink. "And what plan would that be?" "When Ava and Lazarus meet, believe me, it will not be the same. Lazarus knows that Ava and I made love, not once, but twice. He will reject her and it will bring us closer," Julius said, taking a sip of his drink. "What if you're wrong?" "Trust me John, Lazarus is a fool. He will turn her away and look at her as if she's unwanted trash," Julius said, with a deceitful grin on his face.

Lazarus sat on the couch, drinking a bottle of wine. He was just about to take another sip when a knock on the door interrupted him. Lazarus got up, but before he could answer the door, Ava let herself in. "Lazarus!" she said, grabbing him and hugging him. "I'm so glad you're home," she said, holding him as tight as she could. She looked him in the eyes and started kissing him. Lazarus pulled away from her. "Lazarus!" Ava said, confused by his coldness. "Why did you come here, Ava? Shouldn't you be with your husband?" Lazarus snapped. "I wanted to see if you were alright," Ava explained. "You wanted to see if I was alright? Well, I'm not alright Ava! You betrayed me!" Lazarus yelled. "No Lazarus! It wasn't like that. I wanted to get you out of prison, that's why I married Julius," Ava explained. "Do you expect me to believe that!? You married Julius because you wanted him. You want your cake and to eat it, too!" Lazarus fussed. "That's not true! I love you, Lazarus, and I will do anything for you." "Anything for me?" Lazarus scoffed, "Why did you abandon me? At the first sign of trouble, you go running into the arms of another man," Lazarus snapped. "No Lazarus, Julius would have let you rot in prison for something you didn't do. I couldn't let that happen!" Ava cried. "So, you're saying that this was all for me," Lazarus said, walking up to her. "Yes!" Ava cried. "Well, tell me something Ava…did you sleep with him?" Ava put her head down. She could no longer look him in the eyes. Lazarus grabbed her by the arms and made her look up at him. Ava gasped, she could barely breath. "Did you sleep with him?" Lazarus asked, squeezing her arms. Ava was afraid, she wasn't sure if he was going to do something to her. "Yes!" Ava said, with tears streaming down her face. "How many times did you sleep with him? Did you sleep with him twice?" Lazarus said, shaking her. "Yes, yes!" Ava said, crying. Lazarus looked at her in disbelief and then let her go. "Lazarus, please listen to me, I had no choice!" Ava admitted. "Oh, you had a choice, Ava," Lazarus said, shaking his head. "Lazarus, please forgive me!" Ava cried. "Go home to your husband, Ava. It's Julius you love, not me," Lazarus said, turning his back to her. "You're wrong Lazarus, it's you I love," Ava said, touching his back. Lazarus turned to face her with tears in his eyes. "If it's me you love, why are you still wearing his ring? Better yet, Ava do you plan to divorce him now that I'm out?" Ava put her head down. She had no intentions of divorcing Julius. "I didn't think so," Lazarus said, walking away. "I never meant to hurt you," Ava said, turning him around to face her. "Just leave, Ava. I never want to see you again," he said bitterly. "You can't mean that!" Ava cried. "What? Do you expect me to share you? If you love me, Ava, you will leave Julius," Lazarus snapped. "I can't do that," Ava admitted. Lazarus let out a scornful laugh. "I was such a fool. All I was to you was some pawn in a game." "That's not true!" Ava assured him. "Look Ava, I'm tired and I need some rest. So you'll understand if I don't see you out," he then left out, closing the bedroom door behind him. Ava was in tears. She looked around the house that was once hers and walked out.

Julius and John sat at his desk, sorting through stacks of paper. He heard the front door slam and the sound of someone running upstairs. He realized that it was Ava. "Sounds like your wife is home," John said, not taking his eyes off his paper work. "Yeah and it sounds like things didn't go the way she had planned," Julius added. "Well, if you want to check on her, I will finish up and let myself out," John assured him. "Thanks John," Julius said, getting up and leaving. "Ava!" Julius said, letting himself into their bedroom. Ava was there, lying on the bed in tears. "Is everything alright?" he asked, sitting next to her and comforting her. Ava sat up in the bed and stared at him for a second. "I messed up, Julius," Ava began. "How so?" Julius asked. "I lied to you. I told you that I was going to the store to get a few things, but instead, I went to see Lazarus," Ava confessed. "I see," Julius said, getting up and walking away. "I'm so sorry, Julius. I was wrong for lying." "So, what happened?" Julius asked. "We argued and bad things were said, and I don't think he will ever forgive me for what I've done." "So, what did you tell him about us?" Julius asked. "Lazarus knows that I'm committed to this marriage," Ava assured him. Julius smiled at her and touched her face. "Ava, I don't expect your feelings to go away overnight. All I ask is that you give this marriage a chance. I promise, I will make you so happy," Julius said, grabbing her face into his hands. He then leaned over and kissed her passionately.

Chapter 12

The next day, Ava stayed in bed until noon. When Julius noticed that she didn't come down for breakfast or lunch, he went upstairs to check on her. Julius walked into their bedroom, he found Ava lying in bed. "Hey baby," he said, touching her hair. "Are you alright?" "No, I feel sick to my stomach. I've been throwing up all morning," Ava admitted. "You're probably coming down with something. I'm calling the doctor," Julius said, grabbing the phone. "No Julius, I'm sure it'll pass," Ava said, pulling on the cord. Julius ignored his wife's plea and asked for Dr. Peterson. "Is this Julius?" the woman on the other line asked. "Yes Jamie, this is Julius," Julius said, laughing. "Okay, let me get her for you," Jamie said. "Well, I was wondering when I would hear from you," Dr. Peterson said, when she picked up the phone. "Well, you know I just got married," Julius explained. "Yes, I know, and I'm sorry that I wasn't able to make it to your wedding." "It's cool, I know you had some business to take care of." "So, what can I do for you?" Dr. Peterson asked. "Well, my wife is a little under the weather, I was hoping you could squeeze her in." "Sure, can you get her here in an hour?" "Yeah, I will have my driver get her there." "Okay, I will see her then." "Thanks Kathy, I owe you one," Julius said, hanging up the phone. Ava looked at Julius annoyed, but knew he wouldn't take no for an answer.

Meanwhile, Lazarus was stretched out on the couch, watching TV. He was just about to change the channel when a knock on the door distracted him. "Who is it?" he asked. "It's Marline." Lazarus opened the door and there was Marline, holding a plate in her hands. "Hey Mom," Lazarus said, trying to crack a smile. "I brought you something to eat," Marline said, setting the plate of food down. "Thanks, but I'm not really hungry." "Lazarus, you have to eat. This behavior of yours is only going to make you sick," Marline fussed. Lazarus grabbed the plate of food and took the foil off so he could try to force himself to eat it. "Have you talked to Ava yet?" Marline asked. "Yeah," Lazarus said, taking a bite of his food. "Well?" "Mom, Ava made it perfectly clear that it's Julius she wants," Lazarus said bitterly. "I don't believe that! Ava loves you Lazarus," Marline argued. Lazarus let out a scoff. "If Ava loves me so much, then why did she betray me and marry Julius?" Lazarus asked. "Lazarus, Ava was forced to marry Julius. From the time you went to jail, he played on her fears and insecurities. Ava worried day and night, not wanting to eat, not sleeping. Julius threatened to ruin your life, and worse than that, he said he would have some men rape you." When Lazarus heard Marline's last words, he looked at her stunned. "You mean to tell me, he threatened to have me raped?" Lazarus asked angrily. "Yes, and Ava was terrified," Marline explained. "Oh my God! Ava tried to explain, but me and my pride wouldn't listen. I must have played right into Julius' plan. He knew that I would reject her, Mom, and that rejection probably sent her deeper into his arms," Lazarus said, letting out a sigh.

Ava sat patiently in the examination room, waiting for the results of her tests. When Dr. Peterson walked in, she stood there looking over Ava's chart. "So, is everything alright?" Ava asked. "Yes, blood work came back fine. Your blood pressure was slightly high, but I'm not concerned. However, you are pregnant," Dr. Peterson explained. "Pregnant!" Ava said, surprised. "Yes, I take it this wasn't planned? "No!" Ava said, getting up. "Do you need a minute?" Dr. Peterson asked. "No, I'm fine. How far along am I, doc?" "Well, according to your last menstrual cycle, you're about 8 weeks along." "That's two months," Ava said, gasping for air. "Are you alright?" "I'm fine!" Ava snapped. "I tell you what, why don't we do an ultrasound to see how the baby is doing and maybe you'll feel better about the whole thing,"

Dr. Peterson said. Ava nodded her head and watched the doctor as she left her room.

Ava sat in the back of the limo, trying to gather her thoughts. She picked up her cell phone and began dialing a number. When the person answered, Ava just burst into tears. "Ava, is that you?" Lily asked. "Yes," Ava said, between sobs. "What's wrong?" Lily asked. "Lily, could you please come by the house tonight? I could really use a friend," Ava admitted. "Sure, give me 10 minutes to throw something on and I will be right there," Lily said. Ava hung up the phone and buried her face in her hands.

When Ava saw that she was almost to the house, she took out a mirror and began fixing her makeup. After all, she did not want Julius to know she had been crying. The limo pulled up to the house and before her limo driver could get out and help her out, she dashed out of the limo into the house. Ava came in, and to her surprise, Julius had guests over. "Hey baby, it took you long enough," Julius said, kissing her. "Sorry, she ran a few tests on me," Ava said, trying to smile. "Was everything alright?" "Can we discuss that later? I'm a little exhausted," Ava admitted. "Okay," Julius said. "Well, you go and get some rest, and I will be up later to check on you." "You sure you don't mind?" "No, trust me, you would be so bored around these people anyway," he said, assuring her that it would be okay. "Oh, by the way, Lily is stopping by tonight. Please send her up when she comes," Ava said. "I sure will," he said, kissing her. Ava went up the stairs, into her room. After taking a shower, Ava sat on the bed, thinking about her situation. Moments later, she received a knock on the door. It was Lily. When Ava saw Lily, she immediately burst into tears. "What's wrong?" Lily said, hugging her. "Everything, Lily. My life is so screwed up. I don't know where to begin." "Well, start from the beginning," Lily suggested. "I know you girls feel like I've shut you out," Ava began. "Well, we were just shocked that you married Julius." "I married Julius because he blackmailed me," Ava admitted. "Are you serious? Blackmailed you how?" "Well, he threatened to have Lazarus hurt while he was in jail." "I don't understand. If Julius did this, and Lazarus is out, why are you still here?" "Because I know that Julius will do everything in his power to hurt him and I can't live with that," Ava admitted. "No, no, there is more to this, isn't there? You have fallen for him, haven't you?" Lily asked. "Yes Lily, I love him." "Do you love him the way you love Lazarus?" "No. I will never love any man the way I love Lazarus," Ava confessed. "Okay then, go to Lazarus and ask for forgiveness. I'm sure he will take you back." "I tried to reason with Lazarus, but he hates me for what I've done. Besides, I can't go through another divorce, it's too painful." "Well, your life really sounds complicated." "You have no idea," Ava said, shaking her head. "Is there something more?" Lily asked. "Yes, I found out today that I'm pregnant with Lazarus' baby." "What? Are you serious? Well, this is a sign, Ava, that you belong with Lazarus," Lily argued. "No Lily, I can't get back with Lazarus!" Ava snapped. "I don't understand you. You are in love with Lazarus, more than you could possibly love Julius, you're pregnant with Lazarus' child, and you still refuse to be with him. This doesn't make sense," Lily argued. Ava covered her face in shame. "I just can't, okay?" Ava snapped. "Wait a minute. You are afraid of Julius, aren't you?" Lily said, grabbing her arm and demanding an answer. "Lily, Julius is a powerful man, and if you're smart, you don't cross him," Ava said, walking away from her friend. "Ava, if you want my opinion, get back with your true love. You have to remember that what you and Lazarus have is pure, and this with Julius is built on selfishness, jealousy and control. Somehow, you have to get from under the control of Julius and live your life. This baby deserves both of its parents," Lily argued. Lily grabbed her friend and gave her a hug. Just then, Julius came in the room. When he saw them hugging, and Ava crying, he knew something was wrong. "Is everything alright?" he asked. Ava looked at Lily and then at her husband. "Well, I have to get going. Call me if you need anything," Lily said, rubbing Ava's arm. Lily said bye to Julius and walked out. Ava looked at Julius and tried to wipe the tears from her eyes quickly, hoping that he wouldn't notice her crying. "Is everything alright?" Julius asked again. "Yeah, I'm just tired," Ava said, trying to walk away. Julius grabbed her arm before she had the chance. "Ava, what's going on?" he asked. "Nothing," Ava lied. "Ava, please don't lie to me." Ava put her head down and walked over to the window. "I'm pregnant," she blurted out. "You're what?" Julius asked.

"I'm pregnant, Julius," Ava repeated. "But we just…I don't understand," Julius said confused. "I'm two months, Julius," Ava admitted. "That means…" "The baby is Lazarus'," Ava said, finishing his sentence. Julius sat down and buried his face in his hands. "Ava, I thought you were on the pill! How could you let this happen?" he fussed. "I was on the pill, but I guess God had a different plan," Ava explained. "God, huh?" Julius scoffed. Julius continued sitting there, deep in thought. "Julius, please say something," Ava pleaded. "What do you want me to say? That I'm happy when I'm not?" Julius snapped. "I want you to say that everything is going to be alright. That you will not try to force me to abort this baby, because I won't!" Ava cried. "Come here," Julius said, holding her in his arms. "I would never tell you to do something like that. I promise that I will accept this baby as if it were mine," Julius said. Ava looked at him, shocked. "Are you sure? I know this can't be easy for you." "No, it's not! I wish it was my baby you are carrying," Julius said, looking disappointed. "Julius, I just find it hard to believe that you want to be a part of this baby's life. We both know how you feel about Lazarus. Do you really think you could put your hate for Lazarus to the side and really love his child?" "As long as I have you, I can do anything," he said, hugging her and pretending he was fine with the situation.

The next day, Ava got up early. She wanted to see Lazarus and tell him about the baby. She fixed herself up, wearing a beautiful blouse with a pinstripe skirt. She wore her hair down, just the way Lazarus liked it, and put on a little makeup. When she made it downstairs, she noticed that Julius was already gone. "Mary!" Ava called out. "Yes ma'am?" Mary said, coming out of the kitchen. "I'm going out for a little while. Please prepare some steaks with mashed potatoes and green beans for dinner tonight," Ava said, grabbing her purse. "Yes ma'am," Mary said, seeing her out the door.

Chapter 13

Lazarus was lying on the bed, looking at a photo of Ava. When he heard a knock on the front door, he put the picture in the drawer and answered the door. "Ava!" he said, surprised. "Hi! I know I'm the last person on earth you want to see, but I was hoping we could talk," Ava said, trying not to cry. "Come in," Lazarus said, motioning her in. Lazarus and Ava stood there in silence. He noticed how beautiful she looked, and he wanted so badly to take her in his arms and make love to her. Ava tried hard not to look in his eyes, because he was so gorgeous, and she knew that she would do something that she would regret later. They broke the silence and called each other's name at the same time. "You first," Ava insisted. "Ava, I just want to apologize for the way I acted. I didn't mean any of those things that I said. I was just so angry and hurt. I know that Julius threaten to hurt me, and you were scared. But baby, we had something so real before Julius came in and tore it apart. All we have to do is start over," Lazarus pleaded. "Lazarus, we will never have peace together. Julius would never let that happen. He'd find some way to ruin it again." "Ava, I'm not afraid of Julius's threats." "Well, you don't know him like I know him. When Julius wants something, he will do whatever it takes to get it. And I'm what he wants, Lazarus. He will fight you and try to destroy you, and I can't let that happen." "Can you see, Ava, that I don't care what he takes from me as long as I have you?" Lazarus said, grabbing her face. Ava pulled away from him and walked away. "Well, it's obvious you didn't come here to reconcile, so why did you come here, Ava?" Lazarus asked. "I came here to tell you something," Ava said, trying to keep her composure. "Are you alright?" Lazarus asked. "I have to use the bathroom," Ava said, running out of the room.

Julius sat at the restaurant in deep thought. "So, what's new with you?" John asked. "Nothing," Julius said, trying to get him to drop the subject. "Well, that nothing sure seems like something," Marcus added. "Look, I'm fine, just drop it!" Julius snapped. "Okay, but it's not like you to cancel meetings like you did this morning," John fussed. "I have a lot on my mind, John. I just needed some time to think," Julius said, sipping his wine. "Is it Ava? And before you tell me to drop it again, you said she went to the doctor yesterday," John said, trying not to upset his brother. "She's pregnant!" Julius said angrily. John and Marcus gave each other a surprised look and then looked at Julius. "I know you're wondering, and yes it's Lazarus' baby," Julius said, taking another drink of wine. Marcus and John were very surprised and lost for words. "Is she willing to stay in the marriage?" Marcus asked. "Yes, but he is a part of that now. What do I have to do to get rid of that punk?" Julius snapped. "Look Julius, if Ava is staying, that should tell you that she wants you and not him," John said, trying to encourage him. "I don't know, John. He has this hold on her. It's like when he's there, nobody else exists." "So, are you saying that she is still in love with the dude?" Marcus asked. "Yes!" Julius admitted. "Man, that must be hard, loving a woman whose heart is divided," John said, shaking his head. "Well, maybe he doesn't feel the same way about her," Marcus suggested. "Trust me Marcus, he loves her just as much as I love her," Julius said, staring out the window. "So, what's the plan? Because I know you have one," John asked. "I plan to love my wife and this baby," Julius said, trying to convince them.

Ava held her hair back to keep it from falling into the toilet. She had been throwing up for a few minutes. "Ava, you sound sick. Are you okay?" Lazarus said, knocking on the door. "I'm fine," Ava said, flushing the toilet. She grabbed her old toothbrush, brushed her teeth, and splashed water on her face. When she came out, Lazarus was sitting on the couch, looking worried. "Are you sure you're okay? Would you like me to drive you to the hospital?" "No, it's fine, just morning sickness," Ava explained. "Morning sickness?" Lazarus said, confused. "I'm pregnant, Lazarus," Ava confessed. Lazarus got up and paced the floor. "Is it Julius'?" "No. It's yours. I'm two months along. We must have gotten pregnant some time after our honeymoon," Ava said, smiling. "Wow!" Lazarus said, rubbing his head. "I took an ultrasound, if you would like to see the baby," she said, handing him the picture. Lazarus looked at the picture and then at Ava, who was standing there waiting for his acceptance of their baby. "It's really a baby in there," Lazarus said, rubbing her stomach. "Yes," Ava said, smiling. He grabbed her up to him and hugged her. "Oh, thank you, God, thank you!" he shouted. He started kissing Ava. Ava pulled away from Lazarus and put her head down. "I'm sorry, Ava," Lazarus said. "It's fine," Ava assured him. "So, where does this leave us? Because, I'm sure you know that I want to be a part of my baby's life." "I want you to be a part of your baby's life, too. We will share custody." "Custody! Ava, that's not enough. We are a family now and I believe that God is telling us something here." "Lazarus, I have no choice, I'm married." "Well, that can be fixed, you know." "Lazarus, please!" "No. I have been way too lenient with this whole situation and I'm done doing that!" Lazarus snapped. Ava walked away from him and stared out the window. "Do you still love me, Ava?" Lazarus asked. "Of course I still love you," Ava admitted. He turned her around and saw tears in her eyes. He also noticed that it was hard for her to look at him. "Look at me, Ava," he said, grabbing her face. Ava looked up at him and put her head back down. Lazarus realized that she was fighting her desire to be with him. He pulled her closer to him, and he could hear her heart beating out of control. "You can't look at me, can you? You're afraid to be around me right now, aren't you?" he said, stroking her hair. Ava closed her eyes and exhaled. Just the scent of him, the sound of his voice, had her mesmerized. "Please don't," she said, trying to pull away. But he wouldn't let her. He pulled her closer to him. Tears fell from Ava's face as she tried desperately not to kiss him. "I can't do this," Ava cried. "You sure you don't want to?" he said, tempting her. Ava looked up at him and he was so handsome. Lazarus knew that she couldn't resist him, and his plan was to get her to kiss him. Ava could not resist his gorgeous looks any longer. She put her hand on his face and started kissing him. The kiss got very passionate and he picked her up and took her into the bedroom, where they made love. After they made love, Ava lay there, feeling guilty. Ava got up and started putting her clothes on. "What are you doing?" Lazarus asked. "I'm leaving. This was a mistake," Ava said, buttoning her blouse. "How can you say that?" Lazarus asked. "Because I'm married, Lazarus, and this is a sin before God," Ava snapped. "In God's eyes you are still my wife," Lazarus argued. "Okay, well you explain that to him on judgment day," Ava said, grabbing her shoe. "Ava, we did nothing wrong!" "Are you crazy? I don't know how I let you talk me into this." "Hey! You wanted it just as much as I did," Lazarus snapped. Ava looked at him and rolled her eyes. She headed for the front door. Lazarus wrapped a sheet around his naked body and followed her out the door. "Wait!" he said, grabbing her arm. "Don't leave like this," he pleaded with her. Ava let out a sigh. "You're right, fighting about this won't change anything," Ava agreed. "I love you Ava and I would never do anything to hurt you. But, if you think for one second that I'm not going to fight for us, you're crazy." He stroked her face and tried to kiss her. Ava turned away from him and began to walk away, but something startled her. It was Julius, standing outside and leaning on the limousine, watching everything. When Lazarus saw the look on Ava's face, he looked to see what it was that had her startled. Julius stood there, not saying a word, but he looked at Lazarus with hate. Ava's mouth dropped open when she saw her husband's expression. She slowly walked to the limo and got in. Julius looked back at Lazarus again, gave him another hate-filled look, and got into the limo.

During the ride home Ava tried not to look her husband in the face. She had just betrayed him and he knew it. When she got enough courage to look at him, he had an angry look on his face. Ava became very fearful. She knew it was a mistake to cross him. She wanted to say something, but the look on his face kept her silent.

When they made it home, Julius got out of the limo and headed for the house. Ava followed behind him and closed the front door. When they were both inside, he turned around and slapped her. Ava grabbed her throbbing face and started crying. "I'm sorry!" Ava said.

"You're sorry you got caught," Julius snapped. "No Julius, I didn't mean for this to happen," Ava said, pleading with him. "Let me guess, you tripped and ended up in bed with him?" "Julius, it just happened!" Ava explained. "No baby, things like that don't just happen. It takes pulling off clothes, getting into bed, and going through the act," Julius snapped. "I'm sorry!" Ava cried. "I told you not to cross me, Ava!" Julius shouted. "I'm not, Julius. Please just calm down baby, and let's talk about this," she said, grabbing his arm. Julius closed his eyes when she grabbed his arm, because he could smell Lazarus' cologne on her. "You might want to take a bath first. You reek of him," he said, snatching his arms away from her and storming out.

After Ava got done taking a long hot bath, she went into the bedroom to get some rest. She lay in her king size bed and sobbed. She knew that she had pushed Julius to the edge and that it would take time for him to forgive her. She felt guilty, because she did not regret being with Lazarus. She was still totally in love with him, and part of her wanted so desperately to spend the rest of her life with him. When Ava noticed that Julius did not come to bed, she went downstairs to check on him. When she went downstairs, she saw him asleep on the couch. He had been drinking and had passed out. Ava decided not to wake him, so she kissed him and tucked him in.

The next morning, Ava came down to breakfast. Julius was already at the table and he refused to greet her when she came in. "What would you like this morning?" Mary asked. "I'm not really hungry, Mary. Just give me a glass of orange juice." "Yes ma'am, Mary said. "Good morning, Julius," Ava said, trying to get his attention. Julius said nothing. He just kept reading the newspaper as if she had said nothing. "Julius, please talk to me?" "There is nothing to talk about," Julius said, not taking his eyes from the newspaper. Mary came in and poured Ava some orange juice, and pretended not to notice the tension. "Julius, stop ignoring me!" Ava said, snatching the newspaper out of his hand. Mary was surprised at Ava's actions, and pretended she didn't see it. Julius looked at his wife as if he wanted to hit her. He grabbed her by the arm and took her to his office. He closed the door and got in her face. "You want to talk, Ava? Let's talk, baby. Let's talk about how you are playing me and Lazarus like fools. You're just a spoiled little girl that thinks you can have whatever you want. But not this time, Ava. You will not have your cake and eat it, too!" Julius snapped. "You will not talk to me like this." "Why not? Lord knows, somebody needs to tell you the truth. You listen, and listen well. You cross me one more time, I promise you, you will pay the price," he said, storming out.

Later that night, Ava sat at her mirror, getting ready for dinner. Julius was having guests over and she wanted to look her best. She thought that if she showed him how much she loved him in front of his friends and family, that he would forgive her. When she came downstairs, all eyes turned to her. Julius tried not to show it, but he was well pleased with the way she looked. "Oh Julius, you have a lovely wife," a judge by the named Darlene said. "Thank you," Julius said, not taking his eyes off of Ava. "Hi darling," Ava said, giving her husband a passionate kiss. Julius smiled. He knew that he was the envy of all his friends. "You look breathtaking." "I'm glad you approve," Ava said, blushing. Just then, Mary came around with a tray of wine glasses on it. She had a special glass of juice for Ava. "Thank you, Mary," Ava said. "You're welcome," Mary said, with a smile. "Hey Julius, is this your wife?" a man named Calvin Miller asked. "Yes, it is," Julius admitted. "You know what? If you have the kind of taste in business that you do in women, you have my vote," Calvin said. "Thank you, Mr. Miller," Julius said, shaking his hand. "Call me Calvin," he said, shaking Julius hand. He then winked at Ava and went to mingle with the other guests.

At dinner, Ava continued talking with the guests, but her focus was on her husband. Julius noticed her desperate plea for forgiveness, but he was still very upset about her unfaithfulness.

Chapter 14

After the dinner party, Marcus and John stayed behind to talk to Julius. Ava noticed that no matter how hard she tried to get her husband's forgiveness, he was still rejecting it. She became agitated with the way he was ignoring her, so she went over and interrupted his talk with John and Marcus. "Excuse me, Julius, can I have a word with you?" Ava said nervously. Julius let out a sigh. "Excuse us for a minute," he said to John and Marcus. He calmly walked to the other side of the room with Ava. "What is it, Ava?" he asked harshly. "I just wanted to know if you were coming up to bed tonight?" Ava asked. "I don't think that will be a good idea," Julius admitted. "How long are you going to punish me?" Ava asked, trying not to be heard by John and Marcus. "Look Ava, I'm tired of being second in your heart. I know I've done some dirt myself, but I am your husband," he reminded her. "I know," Ava said, crying. "Please Julius, give me one more chance. Please!" she said, grabbing him by the shirt. At this point, she didn't care that John and Marcus were watching. She was desperate. Julius grabbed her arm. "Ava, I'm not doing it anymore! You decided what you wanted yesterday," he said, shaking her. "No! It was a mistake!" Ava said, sobbing. "Really? I don't believe you," he said, letting her go. "Julius, I promise things will be different this time. I love you," she blurted out. He looked at her for a minute, surprised by her outburst. She then grabbed his face and tried to kiss him, but he just turned away. At that moment, Ava feared that she had lost him. She stepped away from him and went upstairs. Julius watched his beautiful wife as she went up the stairs. He wanted to stop her, but he just let her go.

"Dude, what's up with that?" John asked when the coast was clear. "Nothing," Julius said, fanning him off. "Nothing? Don't tell me nothing. In all of my years, I have never seen you reject Ava," John continued. "I agree with John, Julius. She must have done something to hurt you," Marcus added. "Look! I didn't want to talk about this with you, but you already know a lot of what's going on. Ava slept with Lazarus," Julius admitted. "What!? That is probably your insecurities man," Marcus suggested. "No, I caught her coming out of his place with her clothes undone, and he was wearing nothing but a sheet tied around his waist." "Aww, I'm sorry Julius," Marcus said. "Yeah bro, I know that couldn't have been easy on you," John said, rubbing his shoulder. "It wasn't. I just wanted to rip him apart," Julius said angrily. "So, let her be with the dude. You said she still loved him, she's carrying his baby, and now she's sleeping with him. How much more of this will you take, Julius?" John argued. "I don't know," Julius admitted. "I don't know, she looked to me like she was sorry," Marcus argued. "I think she is. She's been crying ever since it happened." "So, forgive her. You love her, forgive her," Marcus argued. "It's not that easy," Julius confessed. "What's not easy about it? Do it! And then you can have a lot of guilt sex," Marcus continued. "He does have a point," John said, clapping Marcus' hand. Julius shook his head at the two of them carrying on. "But for real, Julius, are you going to give her another chance?" Marcus asked. "Yeah, I just want to see her sweat a little," Julius admitted.

Later that night, Julius came into the room to find Ava fast asleep. When he climbed into bed, she woke up. "You came," Ava said gratefully. "Yeah, I came," he said, touching her face. "Julius, I know I messed up, but I promise you that I will never take you for granted ever again," Ava said, touching his face. "I want to have faith that everything is going to be all right, but I don't," Julius admitted. "Julius, I have never kept my feelings for Lazarus a secret. You knew this when you tore us apart, but spending time with you has made me realize how much I want to spend the rest of my life with you," Ava said, gazing into his brown eyes. "Did you mean what you said downstairs?" Julius asked, while stroking her long hair. "I meant every word! Hell, I would shout it from the roof top if I could," Ava said, laughing. "I love you, too, Ava, but I know that you love him more, and that hurts," Julius admitted. Ava became quiet, because she knew that it was true, and no matter how hard she tried hiding it, Julius could see right through her. "Hey!" Julius said, grabbing her face. "I won't hold that against you. I just want your loyalty, love, and respect," Julius said. He then kissed her and held her in his arms.

Weeks passed and Julius accompanied Ava to the doctor's office. Things were going good between them and they were determined to make their marriage work. Ava sat there, going through the magazines, while Julius worked on a crossword puzzle. "Well, fancy seeing you here," Lazarus said, coming in. "Lazarus!" Ava said, surprised. "What are you doing here?" Julius said, getting up in his face. "Well, the last time I checked, this was my baby. I have every right to be here. The real question is, what are you doing here?" Julius grabbed his shirt and was just about to punch him when Ava stood in the way. "Julius don't. He's right, he has every right to see about the wellbeing of his child," Ava said, hoping to calm the two men down. Julius looked at Ava and realized that she was right, and let Lazarus' shirt go. Lazarus rolled his eyes and sat down. Shortly after they sat down, the nurse came in. "Ava Willingham," the nurse said. Ava got up and Julius and Lazarus got up as well. "Ma'am, you can only have the father accompany you," the nurse said. Ava looked at Julius. Julius sat down and had an angry look on his face. "It will be alright," Ava assured him as they both walked to the back to see the doctor. When Ava and Lazarus got to the back, she sat there and waited for the nurse to come in and take her vitals. "How have you been?" Ava said, breaking the silence. "How do you think?" Lazarus snapped. "Lazarus please, I don't have the energy to fight," Ava said, burying her face in her hands. "You're right, I'm sorry. It's just, I thought we had a connection again, and then you were just gone. I can't handle this Ava, I…" The nurse came in before he could finish his sentence. She stood there and took Ava's vitals, and then left. "Ava, why are you doing this?" Lazarus asked. "Lazarus, I can't do this right now!" Ava yelled. "Fine," he said, sitting back.

Later, when Ava came out, she immediately walked over to Julius. Lazarus stormed past her and walked out. Julius noticed how angry Lazarus was. "What's going on with him? Is everything alright?" Julius asked. "Yes, he's just a little upset with me," Ava admitted. "Why, is everything alright with you and baby?" "Yes, me and the baby are just fine. He is upset because I told him it was over." "Really? That's my girl!" Julius said, hugging her. Ava pretend that she was happy, but deep down inside she was devastated.

Later that night, Ava sat inside her family's church. When Jerry walked in he saw her sitting alone, sobbing. "Ava?" Jerry said, putting his coat down. Ava said nothing, she just put her head down. "Are you alright?" Jerry said, sitting down next to her. "No, Daddy! My life is a mess!" Ava said, falling into his arms. Jerry held his daughter in his arms for a while, without saying anything. "Daddy, I know you are disappointed in me. I know I let you down," Ava said, between sobs. "Ava, listen to me," Jerry said, grabbing her face. "I love you, and you could never do anything to take my love away," Jerry said, wiping her tears away. "I wish I knew what to do. I feel so lost, Daddy. How do I please God when I'm married to one man, but in love with another? "Ava, you have to ask God to give you strength to go on with your life," Jerry explained. "I have, over and over again," Ava admitted. "Sweetheart, I'm going to tell you something, and I don't want you to take it the wrong way. You stepped out of God's will when you divorced your husband, Ava. You should never have left your husband for another man, no matter what the cost was. Now, God has forgiven you, but there are consequences for your actions," Jerry said, rubbing her arm. "You're right Daddy, I messed up. Every day, I'm paying the price. I thought about leaving Julius and following my true heart's desire, but I've done enough damage. I can't keep dishonoring God with my actions," Ava said, with tears coming down her face. Jerry grabbed her, and held her in his arms.

Chapter 15

Months passed, and Ava did her best to bury her feeling for Lazarus. She stayed away from her parent's home, because she feared running into him. She saw him at doctor's visits, but she would have Julius right there, so there would be no intimate talk between them. She felt bad that things had to be that way, especially with her due date being near, but this was the only way she could keep what little integrity she had left. She was lying on the bed, rubbing her stomach and playing over in her mind how things would go after the baby was born. "How will I be able to resist him?" she thought. Julius came in, interrupting her thoughts. "Hey," she said, sitting up. "Hey," Julius said, kissing her. "Oh no, what's that look?" Ava asked. "What look?" Julius asked, pretending he didn't know what she was talking about. "Julius, I asked you not to make a big deal over my birthday," Ava argued. "I have nothing planned. I was just hoping we could go out for a little while," Julius said. "Go where?" Ava asked, with a grin on her face. "You know, shopping," Julius assured her. "Shopping, huh? Well, you know I can't resist shopping," Ava said getting up. "Can I get whatever I want?" Ava asked, while pulling his shirt. "Whatever you want," Julius said, smiling. "Good, because I did see this new car that I wanted," she said, walking out. Julius shook his head and laughed. He knew she was just saying that to test him.

Meanwhile, Lazarus worked hard, helping Carmen move her new furniture in. Carmen had hired Lazarus to do some remodeling to her living room. She flirtatiously watched Lazarus and let out a snicker every time he bent over to get something. Lazarus looked back at her, annoyed by all her flirting. "So, Lazarus, do you have any plans tonight?" she said, looking him up in down like he was a piece of meat. "No, I can't say that I do," he said, not taking his eyes off of the shelf he was putting together. "Well, I was hoping you would come to this party with me tonight," Carmen said, giving him a seductive look. Lazarus looked back at her and tried to hold in his laugh when he saw the look on her face. "That sounds like a lot of fun, but I'm not up for much partying these days," he said, getting back to the shelf. "That's too bad. I guess I'll have to go to Ava's surprise birthday party by myself," she said, in a cunning voice. "Did you say Ava's having a party tonight?" Lazarus asked. "Yes, Julius is throwing her a big birthday bash. Everybody is going to be there," Carmen explained. Lazarus stood up as if he was in deep thought. He turned to Carmen. "I would love to be your date," he said, smiling at her. Carmen smiled back with a devious grin.

Later that night, Julius and Ava pulled up to the mansion. When Ava saw all the cars parked there, she looked at her husband with a puzzled look. They got out of the limousine and she realized that her husband had pulled a fast one on her. Ava looked at him and shook her head. "I knew it," she said, hitting Julius with her purse. "Well, I couldn't help it," he said, in his own defense. She touched his face and they started kissing. Julius opened the door while kissing his wife and the crowd all shouted 'surprise!' Ava smiled as she looked around at all the friends and family that showed up. "Did you invite the whole town?" Ava whispered to her husband. "Just about," Julius said, escorting her in. Everything was beautiful. There were balloons everywhere, beautiful flowers, ice sculptures, and a dance floor. Julius had even invited a few celebrities. Ava look at the big fuss that her husband had made for her and kissed him again.

The party started and everything was going good. Ava was really happy with the turnout of everything. Her father, mother, and sister even stopped by to celebrate with her. She was so excited, but then her excitement soon faded away when she saw Lazarus and Carmen walk in together. Lazarus was decked out in an expensive black suit that had gold trimmings on it. Carmen wore a gold dress that matched Lazarus' suit. When they came in, Lazarus stopped one of the servers and got drinks off the tray for him and Carmen. Lazarus spotted Ava and Julius looking at him. Lazarus let out a conniving grin and escorted Carmen towards the entertainment. Ava couldn't breathe, she was so full of anxiety. "Ava, you are making a scene. Get ahold of yourself," Julius said, while gently grabbing her arm. Julius kept smiling, he did not want his wife's jealousy of her ex embarrassing him. Ava tried to control her breathing by taking a drink of her juice. She tried not to show her jealousy, but she couldn't help it. She kept staring at Lazarus and Carmen, wondering if they were in a relationship. Julius began to grow impatient with his wife's behavior and Ava knew it, so she tried to turn all her attention to her husband. She stopped paying attention to Lazarus and started focusing on her husband. "Are you alright?" Julius asked, brushing some of her hair out of her face with his hand. Ava looked up at her handsome husband and gave him a passionate kiss. The guests all cheered and whistled. When Lazarus saw them, he became angry. Carmen saw the look on his face and realized that her suspicions were right, he was far from being over her. After Ava was done kissing her husband, she looked over to see Lazarus' reaction. He looked at her as if he was furious with her. Lazarus kept glaring at her and he refused to hide the way he felt. Just then, their favorite song came on. It was the song he played on one of their dates and at their wedding. Ava became very emotional, because it brought back so many memories. Lazarus was still very angry. He leaned over and asked Carmen to dance. Ava watched while Lazarus and Carmen danced. Tears welled up in her eyes. She couldn't believe that Lazarus would stoop so low as to dance with Carmen to their favorite song. But he did, he pulled Carmen up to him and started singing the song in her ear. When Ava saw that, she couldn't take it any longer, and she ran out. Lazarus saw Ava run out and he excused himself from Carmen, and ran after her. Julius was just about to follow them, but Judge Steffen stopped him to ask about getting together for a game of golf.

Ava ran into the bathroom and closed the door behind her. She began crying and throwing up at the same time. "Ava?" Lazarus said, knocking on the door. "Go away, Lazarus!" Ava yelled. "Ava, I'm sorry. I was a jerk," Lazarus admitted. "Please come out and talk to me?" he pleaded. Ava ignored his demands and started gargling to get rid of the nasty taste in her mouth from the vomit. "Ava, open the door!" Lazarus yelled. "Lazarus, please go. If Julius finds you in here, there will be trouble," Ava fussed. "I'm not leaving until I see you!" Lazarus yelled. Ava finally came out. When Lazarus saw the look on her face, he immediately felt bad. "Baby, I'm sorry…" "How could you?" Ava said, interrupting him. "Ava, I didn't mean it," Lazarus said, trying to reason with her. "You come here and you flaunt Carmen in my face, embarrassing me in front of my friends and family!" Ava yelled. "Is that all you care about, being embarrassed? What about me, Ava? You don't think I'm embarrassed? You don't think you're flaunting Julius in my face? You ripped my heart out and now you got a little taste of what you've been putting me through," Lazarus said, yelling in her face. Ava put her head down. She knew he was right and that he had every right to be angry. "Why Ava, why do you play these games with me? It's obvious that you haven't stopped loving me!" he said, grabbing her face. Ava stared at him with tears of passion, she felt totally helpless when she was in his presence. "Lazarus, don't," she said, in a weak tone. "Do you really want me to?" he said, pulling her closer to him. He started kissing her passionately. Ava tried pulling away, but he kissed her even harder and grabbed her up to the wall. "Lazarus, no!" Ava said, pushing him away and slapping him. Lazarus looked at her, surprised by the slap she had just given him. He became furious with her and punched the wall next to her face. Ava was shaking, she had never seen Lazarus so angry, and when she saw the huge hole in the wall, she knew she was no match for him. "You will regret this, Ava!" he said. Ava was frozen, she was afraid to move. Lazarus then rolled his eyes at her and walked out.

When Lazarus left, Ava put her hand over her mouth and exhaled. She got herself together and went back out to join her party. When Julius saw the angry look on Lazarus' face, he realized that Ava rejected him. Carmen tried comforting Lazarus, but Lazarus was beyond being comforted. "This is a nice party Julius," Marcus' wife, Angela, said. "Thanks, Angela," Julius said, smiling at the slender beauty. "So, when is the baby due?" Angela asked. But, Ava was distracted by watching Lazarus. "Ava, Angela is asking you a question," Julius said, to his distracted wife. "Oh, I'm sorry, Angela. What was that?" Ava asked. "When is the baby due?" Angela said, repeating herself. "Believe it or not, I'm due in two weeks," Ava said, rubbing her stomach. "That's great, Ava! Do you know the sex of the baby?" Angela asked. "No, we want it to be a surprise," Ava said, sipping her juice. "Do you mind?" Angela asked, wondering if she could touch Ava's stomach. "Go ahead," Ava said, smiling. Angela rubbed her stomach and got excited when she felt the baby move. "I'm sorry, Ava. I don't mean to be a bother. Marcus and I can't have children and it sort of gives me peace when I feel a baby's presence." "I understand," Ava said, rubbing her arm and comforting her.

Ava started unwinding and began to enjoy herself again. She spent most of her time talking to her friends and her family. She did whatever she could to ignore Lazarus and Carmen. Later that night, John stopped the music and hit his wine glass with a spoon, to make a toast. "I would like to make a toast to my sister-in-law," John said, hitting his glass repeatedly. "To you, Ava! A beautiful, sweet woman who came in and knocked my brother off of his high horse." When he said that, everyone started laughing. "But for real, may you have many more happy birthdays." "Thanks, John," Ava said, kissing him and giving him a hug. "To you, also, my brother. It takes an extraordinary man to plan something like this for his wife," John said, toasting his glass with Julius' glass. Julius then gave John a hug. Before Julius could say something, they heard someone else hitting their glass to make a toast. It was Lazarus hitting his glass. Fear gripped Ava like a glove when she saw Lazarus making a toast. "I would like to make a toast as well," he started off. "To Ava! Like John said, you are beautiful and sweet. Any man would be lucky to have you in their bed, but you chose Julius. May you have many more wonderful birthdays. And to Julius, an extraordinary man, who gets whatever he wants. I have to admit you are definitely a better man than I could ever be, because if my wife was pregnant by another man, I wouldn't be able to handle that. But you, Julius, you accept Ava even though she's carrying my child." Ava put her hand over her mouth in embarrassment. Julius tried to come after him, but John grabbed him. The guests became restless, talking amongst each other. "Oh, I'm sorry. Your guests didn't know that's my baby Ava's carrying?" "Lazarus, stop this," Jerry said, grabbing his arm. Lazarus looked at Jerry, drank the rest of his wine, slammed it down on the table, grabbed Carmen, and walked out. Tears fell from Ava's face. She was feeling overwhelmed and embarrassed. Julius was more furious than embarrassed. He wanted more than ever to take Lazarus down.

Later that night, Ava lie in bed, crying. "Are you alright?" Julius said, letting himself in. "No. How could he?" Ava said, between sobs. "I guess you can do just about anything when you hate someone," Julius said, referring to his own feelings for Lazarus. Ava said nothing, she just sat up and stared off into space. "Ava, I saw a hole in the wall. You want to tell me what happened?" Julius asked. "Lazarus kissed me and I tried to get him to stop, so I slapped him. Well, he was a little upset that I did that," Ava admitted. "Did he hit you?" Julius asked. "No, just the wall," Ava assured him. "Well, I'm happy for your faithfulness," Julius said, kissing her on the forehead. "Why don't you get some rest? You look stressed out," he said, pulling the covers back. Ava climbed into the bed and lay down.

Julius went down to his office and began to pace back and forth. "How in the hell do I get rid of him?" he said to himself. He grabbed the phone to make a phone call. "Hello?" the voice on the other end said. "Kevin, it's me," Julius said. "Julius, is that you?" Kevin said, sitting up. "Yes, it's me big brother," Julius assured him. "Well, this is certainly a surprise," Kevin said. "I need your help," Julius said desperately. "Let me get this straight. I don't hear from you in eight years and now you call and ask for a favor? Who do you take me for, Julius?" Kevin snapped. "I know, I know. I've been a rotten brother, I know that, but I wouldn't be calling you if I didn't need or trust you!" Julius pleaded. "Oh boy, this sounds serious. What kind of trouble you done got yourself into, little brother?" Kevin asked. "I'm not in trouble. I just have a pest problem," Julius explained. "A pest, huh? Are you talking about getting rid of someone?" Kevin asked. "Not 'get rid of' the way you think. I need you to get rid of a baby." "You're playing, right? I don't know if you realize this, but I deliver babies, not kill them," Kevin snapped. "No, I'm not talking about killing a baby. I'm talking about faking as if a baby is dead," Julius explained. "Julius, I'm sorry, but I can't help you." "I'll give you three million dollars of my money, Kevin," Julius said. Kevin took a deep breath. "That's a lot of money, Julius." "Yes, and you can have every penny of it if you do what I ask of you." "Who is the person you want this done to?" Kevin asked. "My wife is pregnant with another man's child," Julius confessed. "Well, that's some heavy stuff," Kevin said, clearing his throat. "It's not what you think. She was pregnant before we got together." "Oh, I see, and now you are not sure if you could love the child she's carrying." "I wish I could, Kevin, but I can't. Plus, I want to get her ex out of our life for good. So will you help me?" "When do you want me to do this?" Kevin asked. "I want you here by tomorrow," Julius said. "That's such short notice. Wouldn't that cause people to become suspicious?" "No. You can say that you had business here and that you decided to stay here with me," Julius said. "Okay, I'll do it. God knows, I need the money," Kevin said, hanging up.

Chapter 16

Ava sat in front of the mirror, brushing her long hair. "Hey," Julius said, popping in. "Hi honey," Ava said, kissing him. "Are you feeling better?" he asked, holding her hand. "Not really," Ava said, looking sad. "Well, I know something that will get your mind off of things. My oldest brother, Kevin, is coming to visit today," Julius said. "Wow, I didn't know that you had another brother!" Ava said surprised. "Yeah, we don't talk much, with him living in Chicago and all," Julius said. "Oh, I'm so excited! What's he like?" "Well, charming, good looking, and extremely talented." "Wow, what type of work does he do?" "He's a doctor." "A doctor! What kind?" "An Obstetrician." "An OB doctor? That's awesome! I can't wait to meet him." "Yeah, he can't wait to meet you, too," Julius said, trying to force himself to smile.

Later that night, Julius waited patiently for Kevin to show. He had already sent his limousine to get him. When the limo finally pulled up, he ran downstairs to greet his brother. Kevin came in and he was just like Julius had described him. He was tall, handsome, and very charming. Julius stood there smiling. "You look good, little brother," Kevin said, hugging him. "So do you," Julius said, hugging him back. Ava came down the stairs, and when Kevin saw her, he couldn't take his eyes off of her. "Kevin, this is my wife, Ava," Julius said, introducing them. "I was hoping you would say your friend or someone you work with," Kevin said, flirting. Ava blushed and held her hand out to shake Kevin's hand, but he turned her hand over and kissed it. Ava began smiling. "Down boy," Julius said, giving his brother an irritated look. "Sorry, I can't help myself when I see beauty," Kevin said, giving Ava a wink. Julius shook his head at his brother's flirtatious behavior. "Shall I show you to your room?" Julius said, grabbing one of his bags. "Sure, lead the way," Kevin said, following Julius to the guest room. When Julius got Kevin to himself, he let out a big sigh. "Calm down little brother, everything will be alright," Kevin assured him. "I just want to thank you again, Kevin, for doing this." "Well, I need the money. I'm not filthy rich like you. Besides, I can see why you want to get rid of her ex. You got yourself a hot little wife," Kevin admitted. "Yes, so you can see why we have to pull this off," Julius said desperately. "Yeah, I see, and don't worry, we will," Kevin said, giving him a devious look.

Later, Julius and Kevin joined Ava for dinner. She let Mary go home and prepared the dinner herself. She wanted everything to be perfect for Kevin. They all sat down and started eating. "So, why didn't you guys call John over? I'm sure he would want to see his brother, too," Ava said, taking a bite of her asparagus. Kevin and Julius looked at each other. "Well, John couldn't make it tonight. He said that he would come by later this week," Julius lied. "I see," Ava said, sipping her juice. "So, tell me Kevin, what was it like growing up with Julius?" Ava asked. "Oh, you don't want to know," Kevin said, laughing. "Yes, I want to know," Ava insisted. "Your husband was a whiner! All he ever did was whine and tell on everything John and I did." "I was not! He was something else, Ava," Julius blabbed. "Oh, really?" Ava said, laughing. "Yes! He stole every girl I ever tried to date," Julius confessed. "Is that true, Kevin?" Ava asked. "Well, what can I say... my brother has good taste in women," Kevin said. "That's terrible," Ava said, shaking her head in disbelief. "I know. I'm just glad I married you before he had the chance to sink his claws into you," Julius admitted. They all started laughing at Julius' comment.

After dinner, Ava had a few cramps, so she decided to get some rest. Kevin accompanied Julius to his office to talk. "That Ava is quite a lady," Kevin said, sitting down. "Yes, she is," Julius said, pouring them both a drink. "So, I have the perfect plan, and no matter what, we have to stick to it," Julius said, giving Kevin his drink. "I'm listening," Kevin said, taking a sip of his drink. "The forecast says that there is going to be an ice storm tomorrow night," Julius began. "I will send all of my workers home early, and say that it's due to the coming storm. After that, I need for you to step in. If there is some way you could induce her labor, that would be great." "I think I can handle that," Kevin said, taking a small pill bottle out of his pocket. "What is that?" Julius asked. "The less you know the better, little brother," Kevin said, smiling. "Is it safe? Because I'm not trying to kill my wife or her baby, Kevin," Julius snapped. "Yes, don't worry. It is very safe for Ava and the baby. If she takes these, it will make her go into labor," Kevin assured him. "The question is, how in the world will we get her to take them?" "Let me handle that," Julius said, grabbing the bottle. "Okay, but remember, she needs to take only two pills. More than that can kill her," Kevin said, warning him. "Don't worry, I've got this all under control," Julius said, nodding.

The next day, Ava lie around due to early contractions. "How are you feeling?" Kevin said, rubbing her stomach. "I've had better days," Ava said, trying to smile. "Here, let me fix your pillows," Kevin said, helping her adjust. "Thank you, Kevin," Ava said, smiling. "What's going on?" Julius said, walking in. "Oh, I was trying to make your wife more comfortable," Kevin said. "Are you still having contractions?" Julius said, sitting next to her. "Yes, and the way it's going, the baby could very well be here tonight," Ava said, rubbing her stomach. "Yeah, well, this would be a terrible day to have the baby." "Why do you say that?" Ava said, looking worried. "Because the storm out there is getting bad and roads are beginning to close down. I had to send the workers home early, so they could get home to their families." "Well, I'm not worried, because your brother here is a doctor. In the worst case scenario, he can deliver our baby," Ava said, smiling. Kevin smiled back and looked at Julius.

Later that night the storm worsened. Ava stared out the window, looking at the damage that the storm was doing. She walked back over to the bed and lay down. "Julius!" Ava yelled. Julius heard her yell his name and came running up the stairs. "What is it, are you alright?" Julius asked. "I don't want to be left alone, that's all," Ava said, rubbing her stomach. "Are you in any pain?" he asked. "Yeah," she said, trying to sit up. "Well, I'll make you some tea, and bring it right up," Julius said, leaving. He went down to the kitchen where he met Kevin, who was waiting patiently for him. "How is she?" Kevin asked. "She's still having contractions," Julius said, pouring her some tea. He added the pills, that he chopped into tiny pieces, into her tea. "Are you sure this won't hurt her?" Julius asked. "Trust me, she'll be fine," Kevin assured him. Just as he was about to bring Ava the tea, the lights went out. "Oh, this is perfect," Kevin said, looking at Julius. "Take this to Ava and I will get some candles," Julius said, giving Kevin the tray. Kevin then took the tray to Ava. "Julius," Ava called out in the dark. "He went to get some candles," Kevin said, feeling his way through the room. He found an end table with his hands and set the tray down. Julius came in with some lighted candles. When the candles gave the room a light, Ava began to drink her tea. She took a few sips and lay back on the bed. Kevin sat there on the edge of the bed, while Julius stared out the window, wondering if their plan would work. "Oh, God!" Ava yelled. "What's wrong?" Julius asked. "I think my water just broke," Ava said, rubbing her stomach. "Please tell me you're joking," Julius said, pretending to be surprised. "No, I'm not joking, my water just broke," Ava said, rubbing her stomach. "What are we going to do? There's no way we can take you to the hospital in this weather," Julius argued. "Why are you panicking? Your brother is a doctor," Ava argued. Ava looked at Kevin as if she was beginning to worry. "Ava, just relax and tell me when you feel a contraction. Julius, go downstairs and get my medical bag, towels, sheets, and a basin, if you have one," Kevin said. Julius ran out to get the supplies that Kevin asked for. When he heard Ava scream, he picked up the pace. "Kevin, what's happening?" Ava said, crying. "Don't worry, Ava, it's just a little bleeding," Kevin said, while examining her. "Kevin, I feel so weird!" Ava said, screaming out in pain. She then fell unconscious on the bed. Kevin checked her pulse and then waited for Julius. When Julius came in, he saw Ava passed out. "What's going on?" Julius said, in a panicked tone. "She's okay. She is just in a deep sleep. Did you bring everything I asked for?" Kevin asked. "Yeah," Julius said, sitting everything down. "I'm going to perform an emergency C-section, so I need your help, Julius," Kevin said, getting everything ready. After he put all the tools in place, they went into the bathroom and scrubbed their hands with soap. Kevin then started operating. Once he was inside Ava's stomach, he pulled out a baby girl. Julius watched in awe, but he stayed alert. Kevin took the baby and began to examine her. The baby started crying. Kevin lay the baby down on the bed and cut the umbilical cord. He wrapped the crying baby in the clean sheets that were lying on the bed. "I need you to hold her while I finish operating on your wife," Kevin said. Julius grabbed the baby girl from Kevin and began rocking her, while Kevin continued operating on Ava. Julius looked down at the beautiful baby girl and wondered if it was all worth it. He had a vision of Ava and Lazarus bonding over the beautiful baby girl, and thought to himself that it was the right thing to do. A few hours had passed and the baby had finally fallen asleep in Julius' arms. Just then, Kevin came out of the room with a serious look on his face.

Meanwhile, Marcus and his wife Angela drove slowly on the icy roads, trying to avoid an accident. "I can't see anything," Marcus said, trying to see past the sleet. "I think I see Julius' house. Let's just go over there until the storm passes," Angela suggested. Marcus turned the car down the road towards Julius' house.

"Is she alright?" Julius asked, with fear in his eyes. "She is fine. Her blood pressure is stable and she is just resting," Kevin assured him. "I can't believe we pulled this off!" Julius said, exhaling. "Yeah, well, you still need to get the baby out of here," Kevin said, warning him. "You're right," Julius said, covering the baby up. "Where are you taking her?" Kevin asked. "I'm taking her to this family who desperately wants a baby of their own," Julius said, grabbing his car keys and heading for the door. When he got outside, the baby began to cry again. At the same time, Marcus and Angela had just pulled up into the driveway. "Isn't that Julius?" Angela asked. "Yeah," Marcus said, getting out of the car. "Julius!" Marcus yelled. But Julius didn't answer. He quickly put the baby in the car and drove off. "That was weird," Marcus said, getting back in the car. "I know. Where could he be going in a middle of a storm?" Angela agreed. "What's even stranger is that I thought I heard a baby crying," Marcus said, puzzled. "Maybe it was the wind?" Angela suggested. "No. Let's go check and see if Ava's home," Marcus said, getting out of the car. He went up to the house and began knocking, but there was no answer. Kevin watched out of the window as Marcus continued knocking. When there was no answer. Marcus turned around, got in the car, and drove off. Later, Julius arrived home. Before he could get out of the car, Kevin ran down the stairs to confront him. "What took you so long?" Kevin complained. "I had to take my time on the roads. Believe me when I say it's a zoo out there," Julius said, taking off his coat and throwing it on the sofa. "Well, that's the least of your problems. Marcus came by and I think he may have saw you," Kevin explained. "What are you talking about?" "Marcus pulled up as you were leaving, and he looked as if he was yelling to get your attention. He then came to the door, knocking like a mad man." "You didn't open the door, did you?" Julius asked. "No, I didn't open the door! Are you crazy? If Marcus saw me, it would have opened up a lot of questions that we have not come up with the answers for," Kevin said, giving his brother a cold look. "Well, Marcus is not my concern right now. How is Ava doing?" Julius asked, taking his shoes off. "She's doing fine," Kevin assured him. "Listen, Julius, Marcus better be a concern to you because he could ruin everything we worked so hard for," Kevin fussed. "I know how to deal with Marcus," Julius said, with confidence.

The next day, Ava awoke to a pain in her stomach. She grabbed her stomach and before she could move, Kevin rushed over to her side. "Are you feeling pain?" Kevin asked. "Yes," Ava said, rubbing her stomach again. Kevin reached in his bag and gave her some meds to stop the pain. "Where is Julius?" Ava asked. "He was getting showered the last I checked." Ava tried to raise up and it then dawned on her what had happened last night. "Kevin, what happened? All I can remember was that I went into labor. I remember this excruciating pain and I think I must have lost consciousness, because I can't remember anything else," Ava admitted. "Well, you're right. You went into labor and due to complications, you lost consciousness," Kevin explained. Ava looked at him, frightened to ask her next question. "What kind of complications, Kevin?" Ava said, with tears forming in her eyes. Just then, Julius walked in. "Ava, you're awake," he said, hugging her. "Julius, I was just talking to Kevin about last night. What happened and where is the baby?" Ava asked. Julius looked at Kevin and then back at Ava. "She didn't make it," Julius lied. "What!? But I was healthy and the doctor said the baby was okay! How could this have happened?" Ava cried. Kevin grabbed Ava's hand. "Ava, you suffered from what is known as a prolapsed umbilical cord. This happens when the umbilical cord drops through the open cervix into the vagina, ahead of the baby. The cord is sometimes trapped against the baby's body, and the baby is not able to get the oxygen and nutrients it needs. In situations like these, you have to act quickly to deliver the baby. Ava, I did everything that I could possibly do to save you and the baby, but under the circumstances, there wasn't enough time," Kevin lied. Ava broke down crying. She grabbed Kevin by the shirt and sobbed in his arms. Kevin looked at Julius, as he held Ava in his arms. He felt guilty about their plan.

Later that night, Kevin stood in the den, drinking a glass of gin. "Hey," Julius said, coming down the stairs. Kevin said nothing, he just nodded his head. "How is she?" Kevin asked, taking a sip of his gin. "She's better. She's resting," Julius said, sitting down. He looked at his brother for a long time, watching him bury his guilt in his gin. "Kevin, now is not the time to grow a conscious," Julius snapped. "Don't worry, little brother, I'm not about to ruin the plan. Remember, I'm in just as deep as you are," Kevin said. "So, what now?" Kevin asked. "Well, now me and my wife can have the life we deserve. A life without Lazarus. And you, my brother, will be a rich man," Julius said, patting him on his back. "That sounds good to me," Kevin said, smiling. Just then, the smile faded off of Kevin's face. "I'm curious. What did you tell Ava about the baby's body?" "I told her that I had the baby's body sent to the morgue." "In this weather?" "Yes, my wife knows that I have connections," Julius said, smiling. "What if she calls the morgue?" Kevin said, hysterically. "Kevin, it's all under control. I have connections. Believe me when I say the hard part is over," Julius said, smiling.

Chapter 17

Ava sat by the fireplace, staring into space. She thought about the night she lost the baby constantly. It just didn't make sense, she thought. All the months of healthy eating and vitamins all seemed to be a waste of time for her. But, worst of all, she had to give Lazarus the news. Julius came in, just in time to find his wife sobbing in front of the fireplace. "Are you alright?" he said, sitting next to her. "I'm fine. I've just been sitting here, asking God why," Ava said, wiping tears from her eyes. Julius put his head down, he was lost for words. "How are you handling this, Julius? I know you were looking forward to being a stepfather," Ava asked. "Well, it's hard to stomach it right now," Julius said, caught off guard by the question she asked. "I don't know how I'm going to break this to Lazarus," Ava admitted. "Let me," Julius suggested. "You want to tell him?" Ava asked, confused. "Yeah. Kevin said it's not good for you to be out right now, and Lazarus needs to know what's going on," Julius said, stroking her face. "You'd do that for me?" Ava asked. "Ava, I would do anything for you, you should know that," he said, kissing her.

When the roads cleared some more, Julius had his driver take him to see Lazarus. When he got to the house, he walked onto the porch and began knocking. When Lazarus opened the door, he was surprised to see Julius standing on the other side. "Can I come in?" Julius asked. Lazarus looked at him for a second and then stepped to the side to let him in. "So, what brings you here, Julius?" Lazarus asked. "I'm here to talk to you about, Ava," Julius admitted. "Is she and the baby alright?" Lazarus asked. "Maybe you should sit down, Lazarus," Julius suggested. "I don't want to sit down. Now tell me, is Ava and the baby alright?" "I'm sorry, Lazarus. Ava lost the baby," Julius blurted out. Lazarus was in shock. He sat down to take in what he had just heard. He looked at Julius with a furious look on his face. "You did this, Julius, didn't you?" Lazarus snapped. "What!? What are you saying, Lazarus? That I'm responsible for your baby's death?" "This has you written all over it. So tell me, how did you do it?" Lazarus said, getting in his face. "I don't have to stand here and listen to this nonsense," Julius said, walking away. Lazarus grabbed his arm. "I know you did something! I can feel it with all my heart," Lazarus said, looking into his eyes. "You're hysterical, Lazarus, and I don't appreciate you blaming me for the death of your baby. Now, it was your God that allowed this, so don't blame me," he said, snatching his arm away. Julius adjusted his coat and headed for the door. "By the way, don't come near my wife again," he said, leaving.

After Julius left, Lazarus broke down crying. He went into the nursery room that he built for his baby and began tearing the place apart.

When Julius arrived home, Kevin greeted him at the door. "Where is Ava?" Julius asked. "She's in the kitchen with Mary." Julius threw his coat on the sofa and poured himself a drink. "Was it that bad?" Kevin asked, watching his brother's frustration. "Bad isn't the word," Julius said, shaking his head. "What happened?" Kevin asked. "He just gets under my skin, that's all," Julius admitted. "Well, that's the least of your problems. While you were gone, I heard Ava talking to Marcus and the cat is out of the bag. She told him that she lost the baby." "Oh man, did she mention you being here?" Julius asked. "No, but I think he's coming over here tonight," Kevin assured him. Just then, Ava walked in. "I thought I heard someone come in," she said, kissing him. "Are you alright? You seem a little out of it," Ava said, touching her husband's face. "I'm fine. It was just a little stressful, telling Lazarus about the baby." "Oh, how did he take it?" Ava asked. "Not too well," Julius said, taking a sip of his drink. "I wish there was something I could do," Ava admitted. "Ava, it is important for you to rest," Kevin said, cutting in. "As a matter of fact, I would like you to get off your feet right now.

That's doctor's orders," Kevin fussed. "Okay," Ava said, smiling. She kissed Kevin's cheek and then kissed her husband. "Goodnight boys," Ava said, going up the stairs to go to bed. "Thanks Kevin, that was a good save," Julius said, clapping his hand. "What are brothers for?" Kevin said, smiling. They heard a knock on the door. "That must be Marcus. You better go to your room," Julius warned. After the coast was clear, Julius opened the front door and found his best-friend, Marcus, standing there on the other side. "Marcus, what's going on? Why are you here so late?" Julius said, giving his friend the third degree. "I want to talk and it can't wait," Marcus said, storming past him. "This sounds serious. Let's take this to my office," Julius said, motioning him towards the office.

When they arrived in the office, Julius shut the door behind him, went over to his desk, and sat down. "So, what's this all about?" Julius began. "It's about the other night. I saw you leave in a hurry, holding something in your arms," Marcus confessed. "Marcus, I had some business to take care of," Julius lied. "Really? What business is that important that you have to leave in the middle of a snow storm to take care of it?" Marcus asked. "Marcus, I don't run every business decision that I make by you," Julius said, lighting a cigarette. "I see, it was just business, huh? So why are you being so secretive?" Marcus asked. "What are you talking about?" Julius said, puffing his cigarette. "Ava lost the baby, didn't she?" "Yes. I was going to call you. We are trying hard to adjust to this ourselves." "I see. I guess I'm letting my imagination run away with me. I'm so sorry for your loss." "Thank you," Julius said, sitting back in his chair as if he was relieved. "Well, I have to get going. Angela wants me to go to the store and get a few things," Marcus said, getting up. He clapped Julius' hand and headed towards the door. When he grabbed the knob, he stopped and turned around. "You know, there's something else that's bothering me. I could have sworn I heard a baby crying, that night of the storm," Marcus confessed. Julius was stunned at his remark. "Marcus, that's crazy! There is no way you heard a baby crying because the baby is dead," Julius snapped. "Really? You know, I almost thought that maybe I'd been making a big deal over everything that's happened, but I know you, my friend. I've known you since we were kids and I'm not ignorant to when you're hiding something." "Marcus, if you are really my friend, you won't make such accusations," Julius fussed. "I am your friend, and as your friend, I must warn you. If you have done something to that baby, I will find out." "Why are you doing this, Marcus? Why, after all these years, do you turn on me now?" Julius said, shaking his head. "Because Julius, if you continue with these games, you, my friend, will pay in the end. I can't just stand by and watch that happen to you," Marcus said, walking out. When Marcus left the house, Julius buried his face in his hands, trying to think of a way to keep his best-friend off his back. "How did it go?" Kevin said, walking in. "He heard the baby crying," Julius said, closing the door. "What?" Kevin asked, trying to make sure he heard him correctly. "I can't believe this," Julius said, pacing the floor. "Do you think he will tell Ava?" Kevin asked. "No, he doesn't have enough evidence right now. But, I know Marcus. He will dig until he finds something," Julius said, in a worried tone.

Chapter 18

Weeks passed and the emptiness in Ava's heart was still there, over the loss of her baby. Depression began to grip the young beauty like a glove, and there was nothing that anyone could do to help her out of her pain. Julius' attempts to help his wife were all in vain. He did, however, manage to convince John to go along with everything that he and Kevin had planned. Marcus, on the other hand, was convinced that something was going on, and his snooping around caused problems in their relationship. Julius sat back in the kitchen, thinking of a way to convince Marcus to back off. Ava came in and wrapped her arms around him. "Hey," Ava said, kissing him. "Hey," Julius said, caught off guard. "You look like you're in deep thought. Is something wrong?" Ava asked. "I just have a lot on my mind," Julius said, walking away. The last thing he wanted was for Ava to see the worried look on his face. "It's about the baby, isn't it?" Ava asked. Julius looked at her as if he'd seen a ghost. "What did you say?" Julius said, trying to pull himself together. "I was wondering if it's the loss of the baby that's got you so upset lately," Ava asked. "Yes, it is the baby that has me on edge," Julius admitted. "Wow, I didn't know you cared so much," Ava said, caressing his face. Guilt gripped Julius like a glove. His wife had no idea how he truly felt about the baby. Ava put her arms around him. "We will survive this," she said, holding him tightly in her arms. He grabbed her face and looked deeply into her brown eyes. "You know I love you, don't you?" Julius said. "Yes," Ava said, feeling a weird vibe from him. "And you know that I would do anything to keep us together?" "Yes! Julius, what is this all about? You don't blame yourself for the loss of the baby, do you?" Julius looked away, trying to avoid the question. "Hey," Ava said, turning his face towards hers. "This is nobody's fault. You do believe that, don't you?" Julius stared at his beautiful wife, wanting to forget that he was the reason for everything that had happened. "I believe we will get through this and that it is not anybody's fault," Julius assured her. "That's right, honey. We will get through this and that's one reason why I invited friends over tonight, so we can get things feeling back to normal," Ava said. "Ava, I don't think tonight is a good time to have friends over," Julius argued. "Well, it's a little too late. I already made the arrangements," Ava said, picking up a list that had everything checked off. When Julius saw Marcus' name on the list, he became a little nervous. He tried to remain calm, so Ava wouldn't get suspicious. "Marcus is coming?" Julius asked. "I invited Marcus, but unfortunately, Marcus can't make it." A sense of relief came over Julius when he learned that Marcus couldn't come. "You know, I think this is exactly what we need," Julius said, grabbing Ava into his arms. "Are you sure? Just a minute ago, you didn't seem too excited about the idea of friends coming over," Ava said, giving her husband a worried look. "Well, let's just say that I had a change of heart," Julius said. He grabbed his wife up to him and started kissing her.

Later that night, everyone sat at the dinner table. It was John, Kevin, and a few friends. Julius and the other men stood around, drinking wine and chatting amongst themselves, as the women helped Ava in the kitchen. Before they could get comfortable, Ava called them to come and eat dinner. When everyone gathered at the table, Ava said a blessing over the food. Just then, the doorbell rang. "Who could that be?" Ava said, looking at Mary. "I'll see, Mrs. Willingham," Mary said, making her way to the door. When Mary opened the door, Ava could hear her speaking to Marcus. "It's Marcus! He made it after all," Ava said, getting up. Julius could feel knots in his stomach. He looked at Kevin and then at John, terrified that Marcus would put the pieces together. "Honey, look who made it!" Ava said, making a fuss over Marcus. "Yes, I see," Julius said, with a forced smile. "From the look on your face, Julius, I take it you weren't expecting me," Marcus said, taking a seat. "Ava said you couldn't make it," Julius said, giving his friend a stern glare. "Well, I'm glad you made it," Ava said, smiling at Marcus. Marcus smiled at Ava, but his smile faded when he looked at his best-friend. Marcus noticed Kevin sitting next to John. "Kevin, is that you?" Marcus asked. "Yes, it's me," Kevin said, trying not to show how nervous he was. "How long have you been here?" Marcus asked. "For a while," Kevin said, sipping his wine. "Why wasn't I called?" Marcus asked. "Things have been pretty busy," Kevin said, trying to convince Marcus. "I bet," Marcus said, giving Julius a suspicious look. "Ava, my wife sends her love. She is really sorry for your loss," Marcus began. "Thank you. You both have been so supportive during this time. Also, don't forget to thank Angela for me. The flowers and card were very sweet," Ava said, grabbing his hand. "Don't mention it. I know you are going through a hard time right now, and Angela and I just want to be there for you," Marcus said, rubbing her hand. "Marcus, can we please talk about something else? With all due respect, my wife and I are trying to put this behind us," Julius said. "Oh, I'm sorry, Julius. I just wanted to show my sympathy. Besides, I don't think Ava minds me making a fuss over her, do you, Ava?" Marcus said, giving Ava a smile. Julius looked at Marcus like he wanted to strangle him, but he then turned his attention back to his guests.

Later that night, everyone made their way to the living room to have cocktails and talk, but Julius grabbed Marcus' arm before he had the chance to go in with the other guests. "What do you think you're doing?" Julius said, getting in Marcus' face. "Whatever do you mean?" Marcus said sarcastically. "Marcus, this game of yours has to stop," Julius demanded. "No, Julius, I'm just getting started," Marcus said, with a serious look on his face. Ava came in and saw the two men glaring at each other as if they wanted to fight. "Is everything alright?" Ava asked, looking confused. "Yes, everything is fine. Marcus was about to leave, isn't that right, Marcus?" Julius said, not taking his eyes off of his best-friend. "Yeah, I have some business to take care of, Ava. So, I better be going," Marcus agreed. "I'm sorry you have to leave so early," Ava said, pouting. "So am I, but I have a little detective work that I need to get started on," he said, kissing her on the cheek. He turned to Julius, gave him a devilish grin, and walked out. Ava looked at Julius, wondering what she had just witnessed, but before she could ask any questions, he stormed out.

Later that night, Julius sat in his office. "Hey!" Kevin said, walking in. Julius said nothing. He seemed to be in deep thought. "Looks like things were getting heated between you and Marcus," Kevin said, taking a seat. "Marcus is out of control," Julius said, giving his brother an angry look. "For a minute, I thought he was going to say something about the baby," Kevin said. "Marcus has nothing right now. He's just trying to test me to see if I will break." "So, what do you plan to do about him?" "I plan to keep him away from my wife until I convince him nothing happened," Julius said, lighting a cigarette. "It looks like something else is troubling you," Kevin said. "It's Ava. I just don't know what to do. I feel like I'm losing her," Julius admitted. "Why do you say that?" "Because, for one, we haven't been intimate in a while." "Julius, you have the upper ground now. Listen to me, Ava just lost a child. That means she's fertile." "Kevin, what are you saying?" "I'm saying you can give her what she wants more than anything. A baby!" "Trust me, Kevin, that's the last thing that Ava wants. She never intended on getting pregnant in the first place." "Julius, women get pregnant whether they want to or not." "So, what are you saying? That I should trap her?" "Yes! Women have been doing it to men since the beginning of time," Kevin argued. "Kevin, you may be on to something, but I have two problems. One, Ava is on the pill, and two, she is not interested in sex right now." "Julius, I can switch her birth control pills with simple vitamins. She will think she's taking her pills, but she will be taking vitamins instead. And with the sex issue, you are a very handsome man. Make her want you. Take off the suits you wear all the time and show some skin," Kevin fussed. Julius stared at Kevin for a minute and let out a devious smile. "Kevin, I think you might have a plan."

Days passed, and Kevin replaced Ava's birth control pills. The plan was in place, but Ava still had no desire for her husband. She sat in the bed reading most nights, until she got tired. This night, Julius came upstairs to do his paperwork instead of doing it in the office. He had nothing on but a pair of loose fitting jeans. Ava stared at her handsome husband, wondering why he was working upstairs. She continued staring at him, noticing how good he looked with his shirt off, but Julius purposely ignored her and kept busy. "So, what are you doing?" Ava said, trying to get his attention. "Just doing payroll," Julius said, not taking his eyes off of his paperwork. "Looks complicated," Ava said, leaning over him to see his paperwork. "It is, but I'm used to it," Julius assured her. Her desire to be with him intensified when she smelled his cologne. Julius smiled because his plan was working beautifully. He could see Ava squirming. He pretended not to notice and just kept busy. "So, how long you plan on doing paperwork tonight?" "I don't know. Why?" "Just curious, that's all," Ava said, trying to save herself from embarrassment. Julius turned and looked her in the eyes. He saw the longing in her eyes, but still played it cool. "Are you alright, Ava?" Julius asked. "Yes," she said, looking into his beautiful eyes. "Good," he said, turning back to his paperwork. Julius knew exactly what he was doing, he wanted her to make the first move. Ava became a little frustrated. She wanted so desperately for her husband to take her in his arms and make love to her. Julius continued playing things cool. He put his paperwork away and lay down. "Goodnight, baby," he said, kissing Ava. Before he could turn around to go to sleep, Ava grabbed his arm. Julius looked at her and before he could say anything, Ava started kissing him. He grabbed her closer to him, and before they knew it they were making love.

Chapter 19

Weeks passed, and Julius' plan worked like a charm. He made sure that he made love to his wife every night, trying to get her pregnant. They were closer than they had ever been, and Ava was slowly getting back to her old self. One afternoon, Julius, Kevin, and John sat in the family room, watching a football game on the television. When Julius heard the front door close, he went to see who it was. It was Ava. "Where have you been?" Julius asked. "I had a few errands to run," Ava said, putting a few bags down. "Is everything okay? You look tired." "I am a little tired," Ava said, walking away. "Well, I can run you some bath water, if you like?" "That would be nice," Ava said, walking out. "Who was that, Ava?" John asked. "Yeah," Julius said, looking disturbed. "Is everything alright?" "I don't know, she's acting a little strange," Julius admitted. "Maybe you should go check on her," John suggested. "Yeah, I think I will," Julius said, leaving to check on his wife. When Julius arrived in the room, Ava was sitting at the dresser, taking her hair down. "Are you feeling sick?" Julius asked. Ava said nothing, she just turned away from him. "Ava! What's going on with you?" he demanded to know. Ava looked at him with fear in her eyes. "Did something happen? Whatever it is, we can fix it," Julius assured her. "I'm pregnant!" Ava blurted out. "What?" "I'm pregnant," Ava repeated. "Are you sure?" "Yes, I just came from the doctor," Ava confessed. Julius walked over to the window. He couldn't believe that his plan had worked. This would surely be the end of Lazarus, he thought. "Julius, please say something!" Ava said, grabbing his arm. Julius looked at her, still trying to grasp the words that had just come out of her mouth. "Listen to me, I don't know how this happened. I promise you, I took my birth control pills every day," Ava cried. "Julius, please say that you believe me." Before Ava could say another word, Julius grabbed her and started kissing her, holding her in his arms. "Does this mean, you're okay with this baby?" "Okay? I'm elated!" Julius said, picking her up and spinning her around.

Later that night, Julius joined Kevin and John in the family room. John looked at his brother's expression and then looked at Kevin. "Hey man, what's up with you? You have been acting strange ever since you came back." "Yeah, Julius, you are acting a little strange," Kevin agreed. "I'm sorry, boys. I really don't know how a father is supposed to act these days," Julius said, giving them a hint. "What? Did he say father?" "Oh Julius, I'm so happy for you!" John said, hugging him. Kevin came over and hugged him as well. "This is great, Julius," John said. "I know. Now there is nothing that can tear us apart," Julius said, smiling.

The next day, Julius helped Kevin load his suitcases in the car. "I am going to really miss you, Kevin," Ava said, hugging him. "I will miss you too, Ava. Take care of my little niece or nephew," Kevin said, rubbing her stomach. "Don't worry, I will," Ava said, waving goodbye. Kevin got in the car with Julius and drove off towards the airport.

Ava went into the house and was just about to go upstairs when the doorbell rang. Mary came out to assist. "It's okay, Mary. I'll get it. Julius must have forgotten something," Ava said, going to the door. When she opened the door, to her surprise, Marcus was standing there. "Marcus!" Ava said, surprised to see him. "You just missed Julius." "Actually, I'm here to see you," Marcus confessed. "Oh, alright," Ava said, letting him in. They both walked to the living room and took a seat on the sofa. "So, what did you want to see me about?" Ava asked. "Ava, I have to tell you something. What I'm about to tell you isn't easy, so please hear me out before you make up your mind about whether I'm telling the truth." "What is it, Marcus? You know I value you as a friend, and I know that you will always tell me the truth," Ava said. "Thank you for that. That means a lot to me. Ava, I hate bringing up the day you lost the baby, but there are some disturbing things about that night that don't make sense." "I know what you mean, that whole night was blank to me," Ava agreed. "What do you mean?" "Well, I was unconscious. I'm surprised that Kevin was able to deliver the baby under such harsh circumstances." "Kevin delivered the baby?" "Yes," Ava assured him. Marcus got up and paced the floor. "What is it, Marcus? You look as if you've seen a ghost!" "Listen to me, Ava," Marcus said, grabbing her arms gently. Ava really began to get concerned, she had never seen this side of Marcus before. "I believe that Julius may have done something to the baby," Marcus began. "What do you mean?" "That night, when you gave birth, Angela and I tried coming here to take shelter from the storm. When we arrived, I saw Julius with something in his arms. I called to him, but he didn't hear me. He just made his way to the car and drove off. Ava, I heard a baby crying," Marcus admitted. "Marcus, you are mistaken. My baby died," Ava said, with tears in her eyes. "Ava, that is what they want you to believe," Marcus assured her. "I wouldn't make this accusation if I didn't hear a baby crying that night, but I did, I heard a baby crying!" "Why are you doing this?" Ava cried. "Ava! I am not here to hurt you. I'm here as your friend." "If that was true, Marcus, you wouldn't make up such lies!" "Ava! I'm not making this up. Julius had no plans on raising Lazarus' child. Think about it. Julius and Kevin were enemies for years and now, all of a sudden, they are the best of friends? They planned this, Ava. Your baby is somewhere out there!" "Stop it, Marcus! Stop it! You come here, betraying my husband. Where is your loyalty, Marcus? I want you to get out of my house!" Ava said, crying. "Okay," Marcus said. "I didn't mean to upset you. I love you and Julius." Marcus headed towards the door. "One more thing, Ava. If Julius and Kevin really are innocent, then explain why your husband deposited three million dollars into Kevin's bank account." Marcus then opened the door and let himself out.

Ava's mind began to race. She thought about the night she gave birth, and the day Kevin arrived. "Could this be true?" she thought, "Could Julius betray me this way?" She ran to Julius' office and closed the door behind her. She went over to his desk, searching for documents. Just then, her eyes got big. She found a bottle of her birth control pills.

Tears fell from her face as she began to put the pieces together. She found a drawer that was locked. She took a hairpin out of her hair and picked the lock. Ava began searching through his papers and found the information that she was looking for. A bank statement with a huge withdrawal. Ava closed the desk drawer and buried her face in her hands.

Later that day, Julius came home. "Ava!" he yelled out. "You home?" he said, looking around. Just then, Ava came out wearing a red seductive dress. "Hi," Julius said, looking stunned. "Are you going somewhere?" he asked. "Yes," Ava said. "So, where are you going?" Julius asked. "In due time, my love," Ava said, putting her hand to his mouth. "So, did Kevin make it on the plane?" "Yeah," Julius said, loosening his tie. "Where is Mary?" "I sent her home," Ava said, with a vindictive look on her face. "What did you do all day?" Julius asked, walking over to the bar and pouring himself a drink. "I talked to Marcus all day," Ava admitted. Julius put his drink down and turned to look at her. When he saw tears in her eyes, he knew that Marcus told her about that night. "Ava, Marcus is unstable," Julius began. "He made some strong accusations about you and Kevin," Ava admitted. "They are lies, baby." "Really, you didn't take my baby? You didn't have your brother come here and take part in stealing my baby? You didn't pay your brother three million dollars?!" Ava screamed. "No baby, I would never do that," Julius lied. Ava laughed. She walked over to the table and handed him one of his bank statements. When Julius looked at the statement, fear gripped him like a glove. "You lied to me, Julius. You have been lying to me from the start. It was all your perfect plan to get me away from the man I love." When Ava said that, Julius became furious with her. "Yeah, that's right! I still love him!" Ava admitted. "Ava, listen to me…." "Shut up!" Ava yelled. "You don't get to talk right now. You had a wonderful plan, almost perfect, but you never expected that someone would see you. You got rid of Lazarus' baby, and gave me yours," Ava said, throwing the pill bottle at him. Julius looked at the bottle of pills and put his head down. "You had me fooled, Julius. You had me convinced that you loved me." "I do love you, Ava!" Julius said, grabbing her arms. "You loved me so much that you destroyed me!" Ava said, with tears streaming down her face. "I never meant to hurt you. I was just scared of losing you," Julius admitted. "Well, you have lost me. I want a divorce," Ava said. "Ava, please! We can work this out. I promise, I will do anything," Julius pleaded with her. "No, it's final. I want a divorce and you will give it to me. Also, I want to know where my baby is." "I don't know," Julius admitted. "What do you mean, you don't know?" Ava snapped. "I don't know where she is, okay," Julius said, burying his face in his hands. "Where did you take her?" Ava said, grabbing him. "I don't know. A friend gave her to a loving couple," Julius admitted. "How could you do this?!" Ava screamed. Julius tried grabbing her, but she yanked her arm away from him. She walked into the dining room and grabbed her packed suitcases. "Where are you going, back to him?" Julius said bitterly. "Yes, if he'll have me," Ava said. She sat the suitcases down, walked over to him, and gave him her diamond wedding rings. "I will never give you a divorce, Ava," Julius said. "Oh, you will, or you'll be spending the rest of your days behind bars," Ava said. "Do you know who you are dealing with? You will not leave me for that loser," Julius said, grabbing her. "Do you hear me?" he said, manhandling her. "Let me go!" Ava cried. "No, Ava! Now you are going to be a good wife and march yourself up those steps," he said, shaking her. "Let her go, Julius," a voice behind them said. It was Jerry, standing there looking as if he wanted to hit him. Julius let Ava go. "Daddy, I'll be okay, just please take my suitcases to the car," Ava said. "Okay. Yell if you need me," Jerry said, grabbing the suitcases and rolling his eyes at Julius. Silence filled the room after Jerry left. "Ava, I promise you I will find her," Julius cried in desperation. "Julius, it's over. Now please do something decent for once in your life and let me go," Ava said. "Okay," he said, with tears streaming down his face. "Will you let me see my child when it's born?" "Yes. I would never take from you the way you took from me." Ava headed for the door. "Ava! I'm sorry," Julius said. Ava looked back at him and walked out.

Later that day, Ava sat in her old bedroom, sobbing. When she heard a knock on the door, she wiped the tears from her eyes. "Come in," Ava said, clearing her throat. "Hey, I was wondering if you could use some company?" Sissy said, walking in. "Sure, why not?" Ava said, trying to crack a smile. "So, things are really over between you and Julius?" "Looks that way," Ava assured her. "So, what do you plan to do now?" "I don't know Sissy. I feel like my life is a wreck right now. I mean, who screws their life up like this?" "Everybody does!" Sissy suggested. Ava looked at her sister and smiled. "You know, I'm the luckiest sister in the world to have such a sweet, smart sister like you." "Well, that is true," Sissy teased. Ava threw one of her pillows at her, and they both laughed. "It's good to see you laugh," Sissy said. "Only you can bring laughter out of me at a time like this," Ava admitted. "Sissy, I hope when you're older, you will make better decisions than me." "Ava, it's not that bad. You can be with Lazarus now," Sissy suggested. "Sissy, I'm pregnant with Julius' child. There is no way that Lazarus would want me now." "But you still love him, don't you?" "Yes! I will never stop loving him," Ava said, wiping a tear from her eye. "So, tell him how you feel," Sissy fussed. "I can't, he deserves better." "Better than you? I don't agree." "That's sweet Sissy, but I made this choice and now I have to live with it." "You know, Dad is talking to him about the whole situation right now," Sissy blabbed. "Really?" Ava said surprised. "Yeah. He said you had enough stress for one day," Sissy said. "Well, I'm not sure what good it will do. Lazarus must hate me right now," Ava said. "I don't think he's ever gotten over you." "Why do you say that?" "Well, because since you two broke up, he's been on a few dates, but never committed to anyone." "Is that right?" Ava said, feeling a little hope. "Just face it, Ava, he's in love with you," Sissy assured her.

Chapter 20

The next day, Ava lie in the bed sobbing. She felt that her whole world was turned upside down. She opened her nightstand and saw a picture that she and Lazarus had taken on their wedding night, and then started sobbing again. A knock on the door startled her. "Not now, Mom," she said, opening the door. But standing on the other side was Lazarus. "Lazarus!" Ava said, surprised. "Can I come in?" Lazarus asked. "Sure," Ava said, letting him in. Ava wiped the tears from her eyes and began cleaning up the Kleenexes on the bed. She looked at him with tears still in her eyes. Lazarus grabbed her into his arms and held her. Ava held on to him as tight as she could, sobbing in his arms. "Come and sit down," Lazarus said, helping her to the bed. "Your father told me everything," Lazarus began. Ava said nothing, she just put her head down. "Hey, I need you to be strong right now. We have a daughter out there somewhere, who needs us." "You must hate me," Ava said, gazing into his hazel eyes. "No, I don't, Ava," he said, touching her face. "But I must know, why didn't you turn Julius into the authorities?" "Because, I just want to find my baby and just be done with him." "Is that all it is?" "Lazarus, yes! Julius and I are over. I got a call this morning from his lawyer that he filed for a divorce, like I asked him to." "Okay," Lazarus said, in an unsure tone. "Lazarus, my feelings for Julius are dead," Ava assured him. "Good," he said, stroking her face. Ava stared intently into Lazarus' eyes. She was still totally in love with him. He looked at her as if he desperately wanted to kiss her, but he turned away. Ava turned his face back to hers and kissed him. Lazarus got on top of her and they continued kissing passionately. He handled her as if he had been waiting for the moment for a long time. They then started making love.

After they made love, Lazarus immediately felt guilty. "We can't do this, Ava," Lazarus said, putting on his clothes. "What? Why not?" "Because, you're still married," Lazarus argued. "Not for long," Ava assured him. "Yeah, well, it's still wrong," Lazarus continued. "So, why did you do it, Lazarus, if you didn't want to?" Ava asked. "Because I haven't made love since you left," Lazarus confessed. Ava was speechless. She was flattered that she was his only one. Ava wrapped the sheets around her naked body and got up out of the bed. "Lazarus, I will be a single woman soon. Do you think we can start over again?" "Ava, if you show me that you are completely over Julius, then yes, I will give us another chance." "I am over him, Lazarus!" Ava fussed. "Okay, well, I want you to know that I plan on pressing charges against Julius," Lazarus said, testing her. "Lazarus, I wish you wouldn't," Ava said, grabbing his arm. "I knew it! You are still in love with him," Lazarus said, shaking his head. "I'm not in love with him, Lazarus. I just don't want the father of my baby in prison," Ava confessed. Lazarus looked at her, shocked by the words that had just come out of her mouth. "What did you say? Did you just say a baby? You're pregnant?" "Yes, I thought you knew." "You thought I knew?! Ava, I would never have made love to you if I knew!" Lazarus yelled. "I can't believe this," Lazarus said, pacing back in forth. "You gave him a baby, Ava!" "It's not what you think, Lazarus. I didn't plan this…" "How could I be so stupid to trust you again?" "Lazarus, you don't mean that." "Oh, I mean it, baby. I'm done!" He stormed out, slamming the door behind him. Ava tried not to let her quarrel with Lazarus depress her. She went in the bathroom and took a long hot bath. After she was done bathing, she found something nice to wear and let her hair down. She knew that if she wanted Lazarus she would have to fight for him, and she wasn't about to lose him a second time. After she fixed herself up, she headed for Lazarus' house.

Lazarus opened the door when he heard a knock. "Can I come in?" Ava asked. He looked at her for a minute and then let her in. "I was hoping we could talk," Ava began. "There is really nothing to talk about," Lazarus said bitterly. "Lazarus, I know you're angry, but can we at least be civil with each other? We still share a child together," Ava pleaded. "What do you want, Ava?" Lazarus snapped. "I was hoping we could put our heads together to find our daughter." "Ava, Jerry and Marcus hired a detective for that." "I know, but maybe you and I can come up with something," Ava said, sitting down. When she sat down, Lazarus noticed the short skirt that she was wearing. He laughed angrily. "Go home, Ava," he said, opening the door. Ava got up. She turned to say something to him, but he looked much too angry. She put her head down and let herself out. After she left, Lazarus let out a big sigh. It was hard for him, not taking her in his arms.

Time passed and Ava kept her distance from Lazarus. After all, he didn't seem to want her around, she thought. Ava was pretty emotional, because she had just finalized her divorce from Julius a few days ago.

It was a nice summer day, so Ava decided to sit out on the porch and get some air. Her long hair blew in the wind as she swung back and forth on the porch swing. Sissy rode up on her bike. "Hi, Ava," Sissy said, out of breath. "Hey sis," Ava said, trying not to laugh at her sister, who was trying to catch her breath. "What you doing out here?" "Just enjoying the nice weather," Ava said, waving her hands in the air. "I saw Lazarus today," Sissy said, meddling for the millionth time. "Sissy, I really don't care. Lazarus hates me for being pregnant with Julius' child and there is no way I can change that," Ava said, flicking her long hair out of her face. "I don't think he hates you, Ava." "Trust me Sissy, he hates me. Every time I'm around him, he's just really mean to me," Ava blabbed. "I see. I will be right back," Sissy said, taking off on her bike. "Sissy! Where are you going?" Ava yelled. Sissy ignored her sister's yelling and continued on her way. She stopped at the yard where Lazarus was doing landscaping for a man named Bobby Kennings. "Hey, Lazarus," Sissy said, out of breath. Lazarus looked back and put down his shovel. "To what do I owe this pleasure?" "Momma wants you to come to dinner tonight," Sissy lied. "I don't think that's a good idea," Lazarus said, shaking his head. "Lazarus, she's not taking no for an answer." "I don't know," Lazarus worried. "Lazarus, how long will you stay mad at my sister?" Sissy asked. "That is none of your business," Lazarus fussed. "It is my business, Lazarus, because I care about my sister and the baby she's carrying. She is not the bad person you think she is." "I'm not saying she's a bad person, she is just not the girl I thought she was," Lazarus fussed. "So you think by being mean to her, it's going to change the way you feel about her?" "Sissy, it's complicated. I don't expect you to understand." "I understand more than you think. And I also know for a fact that Ava had no plans on getting pregnant with Julius' baby. He switched her birth control pills, trying to trap her," Sissy blabbed. Lazarus had a shocked look on his face. He'd assumed that it was a planned pregnancy. "Lazarus, if you love her, don't let Julius stop you from being with her. She belongs with you," Sissy snapped. "Oh, and by the way, her divorce is final," Sissy said, riding away. Lazarus watched as she rode her bike down the street and laughed, shaking his head.

Later that night, Sissy set another plate for Lazarus. "Sissy, what are you doing?" Marline asked. "I'm setting a plate for Lazarus." "Lazarus is coming here tonight?" "Well, I'm hoping he will," Sissy said, adding the silverware. "Sissy, you better start minding your own business," Marline fussed. "I can't, Momma! Besides, I'm a lot like you." When she said that, Marline looked at her like she wanted to strangle her.

After Sissy was done helping her mother set the table, she went in to check on Ava. "Are you coming down to dinner, Ava?" Sissy asked. "Yeah, why?" Ava asked. "Just wanted to know," Sissy lied. Ava looked at her sister, shook her head, and went back to reading her book. "You know, you would look much better if you took your hair down," Sissy said, taking Ava's hair out of the ponytail she was wearing. "What? Why do you care how I fix my hair?" Ava said, annoyed. "Also, why don't you put on something nice? We are tired of seeing you look like a hot mess." "Sissy, what are you up to?" "Nothing," Sissy said, looking innocent. "Sissy!" "Ok, you pulled it out of me. Lazarus is coming over tonight." "What!?" "Yes, I invited him over." "You had no right doing that," Ava fussed. "I know, but I can't stand seeing you depressed." "I know you mean well, but Lazarus and I are over," Ava said, walking over to the bed and sitting down. "Really? Then why did he just show up?" Sissy said, looking out the window at his car pulling up. Ava raced over to the window and looked out. It was true! The tall handsome beauty got out his car and made his way up to the house. "Oh boy!" Ava said, looking nervous. "Get yourself together, I'll stall," Sissy said, running out. Sissy made her way down the stairs and let out a big smile when she came face-to-face with Lazarus. "I'm so glad you came, Lazarus." "Well, you are hard to say no to," Lazarus said, pinching her cheek. Sissy started blushing. "Hey, Lazarus! Glad you could make it," Marline said, hugging him. "Yeah son, glad you came," Jerry said, giving him a proud look. Ava came downstairs. She was wearing a red sundress with matching sandals. She also wore a light shade of make-up and her hair down the way Lazarus liked it. When Lazarus saw her he was mesmerized. Ava noticed how he stared at her, but she kept a serious look on her face. She knew that she and Lazarus still had a lot to work out. When Ava got to the bottom of the stairs, she walked over to greet him. "Hi," she said, putting her head down. "Hi, Ava," Lazarus said. "Hey Sissy, why don't you come and help your father and me with the food?" Marline said, trying to give Lazarus and Ava some privacy. "You guys don't need help," Sissy sassed. "Sissy!" Marline said, giving her daughter an irritated look. Sissy rolled her eyes and left with her parents. "You look beautiful," Lazarus said, breaking the silence. "You, too," Ava said. "Hey, you want a get out of here?" Lazarus asked. "Yeah, I'll just let them know that we won't be joining them," Ava said. Lazarus went outside to wait for her. When Ava came out, he walked over to the car and opened the door for her. "Thank you," Ava said, getting in. During the car ride, neither of them spoke. Lazarus looked as if he had a lot on his mind. He turned some music on to clear the tension. Ava listened closely to the song that was playing on the radio, and felt as if they were her very feelings towards Lazarus. Tears welled up in her eyes as she felt the distance between them. Lazarus pulled down a road called Kenton, and Ava realized that he was taking her to the beach. When he got out, he walked over and opened the door for Ava, and walked away as if he was frustrated. Ava watched as the frustrated Lazarus walked closer to the water. He turned around and gave her a long glare. Ava could feel her throat tighten when she saw the angry look on his face. "Why did you do it, Ava? Why did you leave me for Julius?" Ava shook her head apologetically. She really didn't know what to say. "I busted my back to try to make you happy, Ava. I gave you all of me, but it wasn't enough!" Lazarus yelled. Ava put her hand over her mouth. She realized at that moment how deeply she hurt him. "I thought about you day and night, hoping you'd come home. I prayed over and over again, that God would let me forget you. Did you even once consider how embarrassing this was for me, Ava?" Lazarus snapped. Tears fell from Ava eyes. She knew she didn't deserve a second chance with Lazarus. "Each night you lay in his bed was too much to bear. I hated you," Lazarus said, with tears falling from his face. "And what did you do? You flaunted your love for him in my face! In my face, Ava!" he yelled. Ava jumped when he yelled. She had never seen him this upset. Lazarus walked away from her, trying to calm himself down. "I tried to protect you from him. I knew he would hurt you. I tried to protect you from this. And now he breaks your heart and you come running to me like I'm sloppy leftovers." "Lazarus, I was wrong. I'm so sorry," Ava said, apologizing. "I thought about you every night," Ava admitted. "Was this before or after sex with Julius?" Lazarus snapped. "That's not fair." "No, what's not fair was you leaving me!" he said, grabbing her arms. "What's not fair is me going to an empty house day and night. Or, how about what's fair to our daughter?" he said, shaking her. "Lazarus, please, you're hurting me!" Ava screamed. Lazarus came to his senses and let her go. "I'm sorry," he said, apologizing. He started rubbing her arms. He looked in her eyes and turned away. "Lazarus, please! Let me fix what I've done to you," Ava said, turning his face to face hers. He looked at her and grabbed her face to his. "No matter how hard I try, Ava, I can't get you out of my system," he admitted. He started kissing her. They continued kissing until Lazarus broke away. "What do you want?" Ava yelled. "Do you want me or not?" Ava asked, out of frustration. "I do, Ava, but I need to know that you will stay true to me, no matter what." "Lazarus, I promise that if you give me a second chance, I will spend the rest of my life loving you," Ava said. "You promise?" he said, pulling her close to him. "Yes," Ava said, gazing into his hazel eyes. He pulled a ring out of his pocket. "Marry me, Ava!" Ava eyes got big. "Are you sure this is what you want?" "I have never been sure of anything in my life, the way I'm sure of this," Lazarus said, getting down on one knee. "So, what do you say? Will you be my wife again?" "Yes," Ava said, shaking her head. Lazarus picked her up and started spinning her around.

The next day, Lazarus and Ava arrived at Ava's parent's house. "Where have you guys been all night? Or do I dare ask?" Marline asked. "I spent the night with Lazarus. Or should I say, my soon-to-be husband?" Ava said, showing Marline her ring. "Oh my God, I can't believe this! Jerry get in here!" Jerry rushed in to see what all the commotion was about. "Lazarus proposed to Ava," Marline said. Jerry looked at Lazarus as if he was very proud, and gave him a big hug. "So Daddy, you think you could marry us?" Ava asked. "Yeah, I will be happy to," Jerry agreed. "Well, we were hoping right now," Lazarus admitted. "What's the rush? Never mind," Jerry said, disgusted by the reaction on their faces. "Sissy!" Jerry called out to his youngest. "What is it, Daddy? I was watching Shark Madness, and the man was just about to get eaten by the shark," Sissy exclaimed. "Well, I think this is more important. Your sister and Lazarus want to recommit themselves to each other." "Wow!" Sissy said, hugging Ava. "Well, are you ready?" "Ready!" Lazarus and Ava said at the same time. "Well, Lazarus, do you take Ava to be your lawfully wedded wife?" "I do," Lazarus said, looking at Ava and smiling. "Ava, do you take Lazarus to be your lawfully wedded husband?" "Yes, forever this time," Ava said, with a serious look on her face. Lazarus grabbed her and started kissing her. "We haven't gotten to that part, yet," Jerry joked. "I'm sorry, Jerry," Lazarus said, apologizing. "By the power vested in me, I now pronounce you husband and wife. Now, kiss your bride," Jerry said. Ava wrapped her arms around Lazarus and they started kissing. The family all cheered while they kissed.

Chapter 21

Julius sat at his desk, burying himself in his work. Living without Ava was too much for him to bear. He looked at a picture he had of her that was sitting on his desk and wondered how she was doing. A knock on the door startled him. "Who is it?" Julius asked. "It's me, Mr. Willingham," Mary answered. "What is it?" Julius asked. Mary opened the door. "Mr. Willingham, you have a visitor," Mary said. "Who is it?" "It's Marcus, sir." Julius sat back in his chair for a minute as if he was in deep thought. "Send him in," Julius said. "I didn't think you'd see me," Marcus said, walking in. "Well, I am a little curious to know why you're here, being that you broke up my marriage." "Julius, you are responsible for breaking up your own marriage," Marcus argued. "Enough with the small talk, Marcus. What do you want?" "I came over to check on you." "Well, as you can see, I'm doing just fine," Julius said, leaning back in his chair. "I also wanted to talk to you about where your life is headed," Marcus admitted. "What do you mean, Marcus?" "I mean your spiritual walk with God," Marcus said, sitting down. "Oh, here we go!" Julius said, rolling his eyes. "Julius, please! I had this dream about you," Marcus began. Julius shook his head, scoffing at Marcus remark. "Julius, God gave me this scripture in the dream concerning you. I didn't know what it meant until I woke up and read the scripture. The scripture was Luke chapter 16 verses 19 through 31," Marcus said, taking a deep breath. "Julius, it talks about the parable of the rich man and the beggar," Marcus said. "I heard of that story when I was a little boy," Julius remembered. "And if I can remember correctly, the guy named Lazarus went to heaven while the rich man went to hell, right?" "Yes, exactly!" Marcus said, getting excited. "Marcus, I don't think I like what you are implying," Julius snapped. "Julius, all I'm simply saying is you have to know the Lord Jesus before you leave this earth, and you have to live right," Marcus argued. "So what are you trying to say, Marcus? That Lazarus has more moral than me, that he deserves heaven and I don't? I know, you think Lazarus is some saint. If he was, he would never have slept with my wife. As a matter of fact, I would put money on the fact that he's trying to get into Ava's pants right now." Marcus put his head down, and gave his friend a sympathetic look. "Julius, I don't know how to tell you this, but Lazarus and Ava got married the other day." Julius looked at Marcus in disbelief and the room became silent. "She sure didn't waste any time," Julius said bitterly. "I'm sorry, Julius," Marcus said. "Sorry for what, Marcus? I mean, this is what you wanted, right?" "Julius, don't be ridiculous. This is not what I wanted. All I ever wanted is for you to be happy." "Well, look at me, Marcus! Does it look like I'm happy?" Julius snapped. "Julius, I know you're hurting right now, but God wants you to come to Him," Marcus assured him. "Marcus, don't you have better things to do than waste my time with fairytales?" Julius mocked. "Julius, I assure you that this isn't a fairytale. God is real and very much alive," Marcus argued. "Is that right? Well, that's you, Lazarus', and Ava's God. I don't need a god. I am perfectly fine the way I am. Your God can't even keep you all from sinning. Look at Lazarus, he is so pitiful. All while I was married to Ava, he lusted after her," Julius fussed. "Are you hearing yourself right now? Julius, you had everything you could possibly want, and you go and take this man's wife. You manipulated the whole situation and you talk like you're the victim," Marcus said, shaking his head in frustration. Marcus walked over to the door, stopped and turned around to face his friend. "I pray for you, Julius," He said, leaving. As he was leaving, he could hear Julius yelling at him. "I don't need your prayers! I don't need a crutch to get me through life like you do!" Julius yelled.

Ava lie in the bed, rubbing her stomach. She was in her last trimester and she was absolutely beautiful. She smiled at the sound of Lazarus coming home from a long day of work. When he came in, he gave her a warm smile. "How is my beautiful wife?" he said, kissing her. "Ready to have this baby," Ava said, rubbing her belly. Lazarus laughed and shook his head. "So, how was work?" Ava asked. "Hectic! Nothing I do for Mr. Rogers is ever good enough for him. He nags about everything." "Sorry you had to go through that," Ava said, sympathizing. Lazarus was comforted by his wife's words, but still had an irritated look on his face as he began to undress. "I have your dinner plate in the refrigerator. Would you like me to warm it up?" "No, I'm not hungry. I'll take a shower and try to wash this day away," Lazarus said, leaving. Ava could hear Lazarus start the shower and she lay back, thinking about how lucky she was to have him in her life again. She decided that she would never take Lazarus for granted ever again. Lazarus came out with just a towel wrapped around his waist. Ava was completely mesmerized with her husband's masculine build and his youthful good looks. As bad as she wanted him, she knew there was no way she could perform her wifely duties in the shape she was in. Lazarus slipped on some briefs and a pair of shorts, and jumped into bed. He rubbed Ava's belly and gave her a passionate kiss. Ava pulled back from her husband, as though something was wrong. "What's wrong?" Lazarus asked. "Are you really happy, Lazarus?" Ava asked. "What?" Lazarus said, confused. "I mean, with this?" Ava said, pointing to her stomach. Lazarus gave his wife a long stare. "Ava, I love you and I love this baby. I promise that I will be the best father I can be to this baby." "I don't want you to resent me later, Lazarus, if this baby looks like Julius," Ava cried. "Ava, I don't care. Right now, I have everything I want. I have God back in my life. I have my beautiful wife and a baby on the way. Marcus and the detective is hot on the trail of finding our daughter. Baby, we are going to have the family we always wanted. Now, this baby is just as much a part of you as it is Julius. Ava, nothing can ruin this for us now" he said, rubbing her arm. "I love you so much," Ava said, holding him in her arms. "I love you, too," Lazarus said, kissing her on the head.

Chapter 22

The next day, Ava woke up at 9 o'clock and Lazarus had already gone to work. She looked over and saw a note on the nightstand that Lazarus had left. *The note read: Put on something special tonight. I'm taking you out. Love, Your husband.* When Ava read the words, she started blushing. She got up and took a shower. While she was taking her shower, a strange feeling came over her. She quickly grabbed her towel and wrapped it around her. She walked around the house, making sure she was alone. She couldn't shake the feeling that something was going to happen, but she brushed the idea off and started getting dressed. After she got dressed, she went over, grabbed her car keys, and headed to the door. When she opened the front door, she jumped when she saw Julius standing there. "Julius, what are you doing here?" Ava said, gasping. "Can we please talk?" Julius said. "No Julius, we have nothing to talk about," Ava snapped. "Ava, please! I can't eat, I can't sleep," Julius complained. "That's your problem, not mine," Ava snapped. "Ava, please listen to me," he said, grabbing her arm. When he got close to her, Ava could smell the alcohol on his breath. "Julius, you're drunk. Go home before I call the police," Ava warned. But he wouldn't take no for an answer. He grabbed her and shoved her into the house. "Julius, what are you doing?" Ava said, backing away from him. "I'm standing up for what is rightfully mine," he yelled. "I'm calling the police," Ava said, grabbing the phone. But when she did, he snatched it from her and threw it against the wall. Ava was frightened by Julius' rage and she didn't know what to do. "Julius, just calm down," Ava said. She tried to make a run for it, but he grabbed her from behind. Julius slammed her against the wall. Tears fell from Ava's eyes. "Please Julius, you don't want to hurt the baby," Ava said. Julius grabbed her face and glared deeply into her eyes. "I want you to gather your things and come home," he demanded. "I can't do that," Ava cried. "You can and you will," he said, squeezing her face. "Julius, don't," Ava cried. "Listen to me, Ava, and listen to me good. If you don't come with me now, Lazarus is a dead man. You got that? He's a dead man! And you know that I can make it happen," he said, giving her a scornful look. Ava was very afraid. She knew how Julius got when his temper flared up. "Just let me go and pack," Ava said softly. "That's my girl," he said, stroking her face. Ava walked slowly to her bedroom. When she got inside, she locked the door. When Julius heard the door lock, he came and started banging on the door. "Open this door, Ava. I'm warning you!" he said. Ava grabbed the phone on the night stand and began dialing her parent's house. "Hello," Sissy answered. "Sissy, where is Daddy," Ava whispered. "Dad took Mom to the grocery store," Sissy said. Ava jumped at the banging on the door and got down on the floor. "Ava, is everything alright? Is that Julius I hear?" Sissy asked. "Yes, Sissy that's Julius. Please go and get Lazarus!" Ava begged. "Okay sis, I will!" Sissy said, hanging up the phone. Sissy threw the phone on the bed and ran down the stairs as fast as she could. When she made it outside, she jumped on her bike and took off. She raced down the streets as fast as she could, dodging cars as they went by. When she finally made it to Mr. Brown's house, she jumped off of her bike and headed up the stairs. Sissy began knocking hysterically. Mr. Brown came to the door. "What is it, Sissy?" Mr. Brown asked. "Where is Lazarus?!" Sissy yelled. "He's in the back. Is there something wrong?" But before he could find out, Sissy ran to the back as fast as she could. "Lazarus! Lazarus!" Sissy yelled. Lazarus grabbed her by the arms, trying to calm her down. "Sissy, calm down! What is it?" Lazarus asked. "It's Ava! She's in trouble. She's scared, Julius is there. I heard him yelling at her and she told me to get you," Sissy said. Lazarus looked at Sissy in disbelief. He ran over to his car, jumped in, and sped off.

"Open the door, Ava!" Julius yelled. "Go away, Julius, the police are on their way!" Ava lied. "Ava, if you don't open this door now, I'll kick it down," Julius demanded. Ava began to shake. She grabbed the phone to dial the police, but before she could dial the number, Julius broke the door down. "Put the phone down," he demanded. "No," Ava said, shaking her head. "I said put it down!" he said, bending her arm. Ava dropped the phone and gasped for air. "Please, don't do this Julius!" Ava cried. "You are my wife and you will not embarrass me any longer!" he yelled. "Let me go," Ava cried. But Julius wouldn't listen. He grabbed her up to him and tried to kiss her. Lazarus came in. "Let her go," Lazarus snapped. Julius let Ava go and let out a scornful laugh. "You wasted no time calling him!" he said, looking at Ava with an evil glare. Ava shook with fear. She was still afraid to move. "If you have a problem with my wife, you work it out with me you coward," Lazarus said, getting in his face. "Is that right?" Julius said, getting back in his face. "Why don't you just leave, Julius? You have no business being here," Lazarus snapped. "I have every right to be here! That's my child she's carrying," Julius yelled. Lazarus looked at him with great rage. "What's wrong, Lazarus? Am I getting under your skin?" Julius mocked. "That's right, that's my baby, and believe me when I say I put in the work every day to make sure she got pregnant." Lazarus became very angry. He looked at Julius like he wanted to kill him. Lazarus punched him in the face, knocking him to the floor. Julius wiped the blood from his mouth, got up, and charged Lazarus. The two of them started fighting. "Stop it!" Ava screamed. But there was no use. Tempers flared and the two men battled their hatred and frustration out on one another. Ava tried moving back, because they were all over the room, tearing each other to shreds. Lazarus punched Julius as hard as he could, sending him falling back into Ava. When Julius fell into Ava, Ava fell over and hit her head on the dresser. Lazarus watched in horror as he saw his wife fall. He made his way over to his wife. "Ava," he said, trying to get her to respond to him. But there was no use, she was unconscious. Julius looked at Lazarus trying to wake Ava up. "Don't just stand there, Julius, call for help!" Lazarus cried. Julius made his way over to the phone and called 911. "Ava, wake up baby, please wake up!" Lazarus cried.

At the hospital, Julius and Lazarus stood around in the waiting room, waiting to hear from the doctor. Just then, Marline and Jerry walked in. "What's going on?" Marline said with fear all over her face. "Ava, she…" But before Lazarus could finish, Marline walked over to Julius. "What are you doing here?" she snapped. "You did something to her, didn't you?" Marline continued. "I didn't put Ava here, Marline, you have your precious son-in-law to thank for that," Julius snapped. Marline looked at Lazarus in disbelief. "Lazarus, what is he talking about?" Marline asked. Jerry tried to calm his wife down, but she was furious. "It was an accident. I was trying to protect her from him," Lazarus said, pointing to Julius. "What she needed was protection from you!" Julius yelled. "You're kidding, right? If it weren't for you, none of this would have ever happened!" Lazarus said, getting in his face. "Stop it right now," Jerry yelled. "The two of you are behaving like children," Jerry continued. Lazarus walked away from Julius and sat down. "What is taking so long?" Marline said. Jerry walked over to her and held her in his arms. The doctor came in. "Doctor, is she okay?" Lazarus asked. The doctor took a deep breath. "I'm sorry, she didn't make it," the doctor said, holding his head down. Marline buried her head in Jerry's chest and wept hysterically. It was as if time stopped. Lazarus was overwhelmed with grief. He went over to a corner and buried his face in his hands. "What about the baby?" Julius asked. "I'm sorry, but they both passed away. My staff and I did all we could. Again, I'm so sorry for your loss," the doctor said. Julius stood there with an angry look on his face. Instead of him taking responsibility for his own actions, he felt that it was Lazarus' fault. Lazarus sat there in tears. "Why, God, why did you take her?!" Lazarus cried. Marline and Jerry then made their way over to him and started comforting him. When Julius saw them comforting Lazarus, he became even more furious and walked out.

Chapter 23

Later that night, Lazarus sat in Ava's room, looking at her photo albums. Tears fell from his face as he thought of all the times that they shared together. He thought about the day when they had just met, their wedding day, times they laughed, and times they fought. A knock on the door brought him back to reality. "Lazarus," Marline said, knocking. "Can I come in?" she said. "Yeah, Mom," Lazarus said. Marline came in and sat next to him on the bed. "I saw the light on," Marline said. "I couldn't sleep," Lazarus said. "Neither could I," Marline admitted. "For a minute, you looked just like Ava with your hair down and all," Lazarus said, trying to crack a smile. "Where is Jerry?" Lazarus asked. "He wanted to get out of the house for a little while, so he went over to Marcus' house. Marcus told him that the investigation is going good. He thinks he's close to finding your daughter. I'm glad to hear some good news at a time like this, you know," Marline said. "Yeah! It's funny, Ava and I were just talking about naming Marcus and Angela the godparents of both of our children," Lazarus said, letting out a huge sigh. Marline put her head down. She knew that Lazarus was in the same hell she was in. "Where is Sissy?" Lazarus asked. Marline cleared her throat. "I finally got her to fall asleep," Marline said. "I tried to protect her," Lazarus said, breaking down crying. "I know you did, Lazarus. I don't doubt your love for my daughter," Marline said, grabbing his face. Lazarus looked at her and was thankful for her support, but it didn't make him feel any better. He got up and walked over to the bookshelf and grabbed a picture of the two of them off of the shelf. He stared at the picture as if he was lost. "I keep playing the whole thing in my mind. I should have called the police. I should have let them handle Julius. I know how much he gets under my skin and how our tempers flare up when we see each other." "Lazarus, you did what any husband would have done. You protected your wife," Marline argued. "Did I, Mom? If I protected her, then where is she?" Marline put her head down. She had no answers for Lazarus. "Does Jerry blame me?" Lazarus said, breaking the silence. "No Lazarus, you mustn't believe that," Marline said. Just then, Sissy started screaming. Marline looked at Lazarus. "I better get back to Sissy," Marline said. She kissed him on the cheek, patted his face, and let herself out. Lazarus stared off into space and wondered if he could survive his wife's death.

Days passed, and the day of the funeral had come. Jerry and Marline wanted a short service, so after they viewed Ava's body, they immediately went over to the burial. Jerry's friend and co-pastor of the church did the speaking and praying. Lazarus was in so much pain, but it didn't stop him and Julius from giving each other evil stares. They stared at each other as if they wanted to finish what they started. Sissy saw how Lazarus stared at Julius, and grabbed his hand in order to get him to focus on his love for Ava, instead of his hatred for Julius. Lazarus looked down at her and let out a weak smile, but he then looked at Julius again, with a hate-filled glare.

Days passed and Lazarus did his best to cope. He lay on the couch, trying not to think about Ava, but there were reminders of her everywhere. He was about to close his eyes and get some sleep, when there was a knock on the door. Lazarus made his way over to the door, and there standing on the other side was Jerry. "Jerry, come in," Lazarus said, walking away and leaving the door wide open. "It looks like this place could use some TLC," Jerry said, looking around at the messy house. "What do you want, Jerry?" Lazarus said, laying his head back as if he had a headache. "I wanted to see how you were doing. Plus, Marline sent you a plate," Jerry said, sitting the plate on the table. "Thanks, but I'm not hungry," Lazarus said. "Lazarus, this has to stop. Do you think Ava would have wanted you to behave this way? You have to pull yourself together, man," Jerry fussed. Lazarus looked at Jerry and buried his face in his hands. "Lazarus, Ava would have wanted for you to move on," Jerry said. "Look, Jerry, I know you mean well, but I'm just not in the mood for company right now," Lazarus fussed. "Alright, but I need you to know one more thing," Jerry said, letting out a sigh. "Marline wants us to move up to Texas with her sister. It's hard for her and Sissy to be at the house with so many memories," Jerry said. Lazarus said nothing, he just acted as if he was in deep thought. "Lazarus, we were hoping you'd come with us," Jerry continued. "I can't do that, Jerry. "Why not, Lazarus? You have nothing here," Jerry argued. "Jerry, I appreciate you asking me, but I'm not leaving," Lazarus fussed. "Lazarus, how long will you do this dance?" Jerry said. "What?" Lazarus asked, confused by the question. "Ava is gone and you act as if we should bury you, too," Jerry snapped. Lazarus rolled his eyes, but it didn't stop Jerry from getting in his face. "Lazarus, we don't want to lose you, too, but I'm afraid if you don't come with us, you'll end up this bitter dude with nothing to live for. I promised your father that I would take care of you, but my promise to God to take care of my wife and daughter takes priority over my promise to your father. Now, I can't live up to my promise if you don't come with us. Lazarus, please, I can't shake this bad feeling I'm having that if you stay here, you'll regret it. Look Lazarus, I love you like a son and I will feel much better if you would just come to Texas with us," Jerry fussed. Lazarus looked at Jerry and was moved by his love for him. "I'm sorry, Jerry, I can't," Lazarus said, walking away. Disappointment gripped Jerry like a glove. "Okay, I understand, but at least come and say goodbye to the family tomorrow. We're leaving at noon," Jerry said, letting himself out.

The next day, Lazarus made his way over to his in-law's house to say goodbye. When Sissy saw him, she dropped her box of books on the ground and ran over to him. He grabbed her in his arms and hugged her. "I'm going to miss you," Sissy said, with tears in her eyes. "I'm going to miss you, too," Lazarus said, wiping her tears. Marline and Jerry watched with great sadness as Sissy said her goodbyes to Lazarus. "Listen to me," Lazarus said, holding her face, "I want you to take care of your old man. You know he's getting old," Lazarus teased. When Jerry heard him, he laughed. "But seriously, one day you will be a heartbreaker like your sister. Make sure that whatever guy you choose is worthy of your love," Lazarus said, fighting back tears. Sissy held on to him for dear life, and without saying anything else, she ran and jumped in the car. Marline walked over to Lazarus. She had on a beautiful flowered dress with sandals, and she wore her hair down, so that it flowed down her back. She began fixing Lazarus' shirt collar as if she was preparing him for something big. Lazarus noticed that she had a hard time looking at him. He lifted her head and when he did, she had a face filled with tears. "Mom, I will be alright," Lazarus assured her. "I know," Marline said, stroking his face. "And I know why you can't leave right now. You got to settle what's in your heart. But when you're ready, you will always have a home with us," Marline said. Lazarus grabbed her hands and kissed them and held her in his arms. "Thank you for loving me," he whispered in her ear. Marline kissed him on the cheek and walked over to the car. "Last chance," Jerry joked. Lazarus let out a smile, but then began to cry. Jerry grabbed him and held him in his arms. "I love you, son," Jerry said. "Take care of yourself," Jerry continued. "I will," Lazarus assured him. Jerry reached in his pocket and pulled out a piece of paper with numbers on it. "If you ever need to reach us, call these numbers," Jerry said, giving the numbers to Lazarus. He hugged Lazarus again and got in the car. Lazarus watched as they drove away, waving until he didn't see them anymore. He made his way home and collapsed on the couch. Depression hit him like tons of bricks. He had lost so much in such a short time, that he was having a hard time coping. Everywhere he looked reminded him of what he lost. He wondered, was it a mistake, not leaving with Jerry? He grabbed his keys and headed out. He thought fresh air would do him some good. Lazarus drove to the beach and lay on the top of his car, thinking about Ava. "God, I can't do this without you," he said, looking towards the sky. "Please, Jesus, take this pain. Help me, please," he cried. Time passed and it was getting late, so Lazarus jumped in his car and headed home.

On his way to the house, he stopped at a red light. When the light turned green, he drove forward, and suddenly, a truck ran into his car.

Chapter 24

Julius sat at his desk, filling out paperwork. He had a knock on his door. "Mr. Willingham, Mr. Smith is here to see you," Mary said. "Thanks Mary, let him in," Julius said, getting up. "Julius," Brian said, shaking Julius' hand. "How are you, Brian?" Julius asked. "I'm doing well," Brian said. "Can I get us a drink?" Julius asked. "No, thank you," Brian said. "Well, please sit down, Brian," Julius said. Brian took a seat and looked around Julius' office. "I see you upgraded," Brian noticed. "Yeah, I got tired of the dark gloomy office. I wanted something with a little more style," Julius said. Julius walked over to the other side of his desk and sat down. "So, I'm curious as to why you wanted to see me?" Brian said, getting to the point. "That's what I like about you, Brian. You always get straight to the point," Julius said, smiling. "Well, it's not every day that you hear from a man of your stature. I figure it must be important," Brian said. "Well, it is important, Brian," Julius said, clearing his throat. "I understand that you bought both of Jerry's properties," Julius said. "Yes, that's true," Brian said, looking confused. "Well, I want to buy them from you," Julius offered. Brian looked even more confused. "Julius, I didn't know you were into real-estate. Plus, a man with your money should want something a little more elegant." "Yes, but my wife grew up there and the place holds special memories for Ava and me," Julius lied. "Well, I wish I could help you, but I can't sell. I just bought this property, plus I have Lazarus living in one of the houses. You understand, don't you?" Brian said. Julius looked disappointed. He nodded his head as if he understood. "I understand if you don't want to sell, Brian, but I would hate to see a man as smart as you turn down a good offer." Brian looked intently at Julius. "This is what I'm offering you for those properties," Julius said, handing him a check. "I'm sure you will find it well over what the properties are worth. It's a generous offer," Julius said. Brian looked at the check and then at Julius as if he was crazy. Julius just sat back with a devilish grin on his face.

Lazarus squirmed in his bed. "Lazarus, can you hear me?" A woman's voice said. Lazarus opened his eyes, but then closed them again. "Lazarus, open your eyes if you can hear me," the voice continued. Lazarus finally gained enough strength to open his eyes. He looked at the woman, who was in a nurse's uniform. He focused his eyes on his other surroundings. "Where am I?" Lazarus asked. "You're in the hospital. I'm your nurse, Pam." "How long have I been here?" Lazarus asked. "You been here for a few weeks now. You were in a serious car accident and you've been in a coma ever since," the nurse explained. She began checking him. "Do you remember the accident?" the nurse asked. "Not really," Lazarus said. "You were hit by a drunk driver," the nurse continued. "What? Did he…" "No, he didn't make it," the nurse said, finishing his sentence. Lazarus put his hand over his face in deep sorrow. He noticed that his other arm was in a cast. "You suffered a broken wrist and also a broken leg. A guy who found you pulled you out of your burning car, and broke your leg trying to save you. You also suffered some head trauma and a few broken ribs" the nurse explained. Lazarus held his head. He felt like he was in a nightmare. "Do you have anybody I can contact for you?" the nurse asked. Lazarus thought about Jerry, but remembered the contact numbers he had given him were in the car. "No," Lazarus said. "Okay, well, I will talk to your doctor and he will be in shortly to talk to you," the nurse said. Lazarus nodded his head as the nurse left out.

Ten minutes later, the nurse came back with the doctor. "Hello, Lazarus," the doctor said. "Hi," Lazarus said, in a weak voice. "Are you feeling any pain right now?" the doctor asked. "Yes," Lazarus said. "Nurse, get me an order of morphine, stat, please," the doctor said, giving her the order. "Yes, sir," the nurse said. "Lazarus, you've been out for a while. We didn't know if you would survive," the doctor said. "How long will it take for my arm and leg to heal?" Lazarus asked. The doctor's face turned serious. "Lazarus, I'm sorry to have to tell you this, but your arm and leg are the least of your problems," the doctor said. "What do you mean?" Lazarus asked. "We ran a few tests and we also had to perform surgery on you, and we discovered cancer. I'm sorry," the doctor said. "I can do chemotherapy or radiation treatment, right?" "Lazarus, your cancer is in its last stage. I'm surprised you didn't know. The best thing we can do for you now is to make you comfortable," the doctor said. "Are you telling me that I'm going to die?" The doctor put his head down. "How long do I have?" Lazarus asked. "A few weeks, maybe a month," the doctor said. Lazarus was devastated. He couldn't believe the news he had just heard.

Days later, Lazarus sat on his hospital bed, waiting for his discharge papers. The nurse finally came in. "Okay, I have your discharge papers. I need for you to sign here. Also, hospice will contact you tomorrow. These are your prescriptions and you are good to go," the nurse said. Lazarus gave her a weak smile. The nurse helped him over to a wheelchair. She wheeled him to the front of the hospital. "Nurse, I will be fine from here," Lazarus said. "Are you sure? It's no bother for me to stand here," the nurse said. "I'm fine, thank you," Lazarus said. The nurse gave him his crutches and he slowly walked over to a cab that was waiting for him.

Angela sat on the couch, watching soaps. "Girl, he is cheating on you," Angela said, shaking her head. A knock on the door snatched her attention from her soaps. "Who could that be?" she said, getting up. When she opened the door, to her surprise, standing on the other side, was Lazarus. "Lazarus! This is a surprise! Please, come in," she said, trying to help him. Lazarus made his way in and Angela helped him to the couch. She grabbed the remote and turned her stories off. "What happen to you?" Angela asked. "I was in a car accident," Lazarus said. "Oh, I'm sorry to hear that, Lazarus," Angela said, holding her chest. "Is Marcus here?" Lazarus asked. "No, he's actually been looking for you. He got a lead on your baby girl. He's been working on this night and day. I told him I knew his schooling in detective work would pay off one day." "So he believes he found my little girl?" Lazarus asked. "Yes, isn't it exciting?!" Angela said, with great enthusiasm. "Yes, it is," Lazarus said, trying to fight his tears. Lazarus turned his head from her as tears fell from his eyes. "Lazarus, did I say something wrong?" Angela said. "No, Angela! It's just that I can't be here for my little girl," Lazarus confessed. "What do you mean?" Angela asked. "I'm dying, Angela. And I only have maybe a few weeks. It's cancer," Lazarus said. Angela put her hand over her mouth. She didn't know what to say. "Lazarus, I'm sorry!" Angela cried. "It's fine. The good Lord gives us life and he takes it away." "Is there anything I can do for you?" Angela asked. "Actually, there is. I want you and Marcus to take care of my daughter. Please, Angela, tell me you'll do it," Lazarus pleaded. "I would be honored!" Angela said, crying. Lazarus reached in his pocket and pulled out a will. "I had the nurse at the hospital make this out for me, just in case you run into any problems keeping her." Angela's hands shook as she took the papers from Lazarus' hand. "I always wanted a child. Thank you," Angela said, hugging him. "You're welcome," Lazarus said, hugging her back. "Well, I have to get going, Lazarus said. He walked over to the door and opened it. "Lazarus," Angela called. Lazarus stopped and turned around. "Thank you, again," Angela said. Lazarus nodded his head and walked out.

When Lazarus made it to the house, he took out his keys to open the door. When he had a hard time opening the door, he looked up and saw a note on the door. The note read: Under new management. New owner, Julius Willingham. Lazarus couldn't believe his eyes. In a rage, he balled the paper up and threw it on the ground.

Julius sat on the couch watching TV when the doorbell rang. He got up and went over to answer it. There on the other side stood Lazarus. "Lazarus, what a surprise," Julius said, mockingly. "Julius, I just got out of the hospital. Please give me the keys to my house," Lazarus said, in a calm tone. "I'm sorry, Lazarus, but the place is being rented out to someone else." "Where am I supposed to go, Julius?" Lazarus snapped. "That's not my problem," Julius said, with a smirk on his face. "Julius, I know you hate me, and I know you blame me for Ava's death, but this is plain cruel!" Lazarus argued. "Lazarus, I have things to do. So if you will excuse me…" Julius said, trying to close the door. Lazarus grabbed the door with his one good arm, to stop Julius from closing it. "Julius, I'm dying. Please don't do this," Lazarus pleaded. "Nice try, Lazarus. Try that on someone who cares," Julius said, slamming the door in his face.

The next day, Julius arose to a nice breakfast. He sat there at his kitchen table, like he always did, and read his newspaper. "Mr. Willingham, it's 9 o'clock. Remember, you have a meeting at 10 o'clock," Mary said. "That's right," Julius said, getting up. He grabbed his briefcase and headed for the front door. When he made it outside, he was shocked when he saw Lazarus asleep on the porch. "Lazarus, what are you doing out here?" Julius fussed. "Julius, I told you, I'm sick," Lazarus said, in a weak tone. "Lazarus, you have to go, you can't stay here," Julius said. "Julius, you took my home. I have nowhere else to go," Lazarus said, sitting up. "Well, you need to be gone before I get back," Julius said, walking off. He made his way over to the car, got in, and drove off.

Later that night, Julius came home after a hard day at work. When he saw Lazarus still lying there, he shook his head in frustration. "Are you serious?" Julius said, walking up to Lazarus. Lazarus lifted his head enough to see Julius standing there. "I told you to leave, Lazarus," Julius fussed. "I'm too weak to move. Please Julius, have mercy," Lazarus begged. "Mercy? You don't need mercy. What you need is a bath," Julius said, covering his nose. "I told you that I'm sick. Look at me, Julius! My body is still healing from the car accident that I was in. I haven't eaten all day. You took my home. What in God's name do you expect me to do?" Lazarus pleaded. "I expect you to leave. Go to a shelter or something," Julius said. "Julius, I told you that I'm too weak to move," Lazarus cried. "Yeah, whatever," Julius said, stepping over him and walking into his beautiful home. After Julius went into the house, Lazarus began to sob. "Help me God! Help me please!" Lazarus cried. Just then, a dog walked up to him. Lazarus let out a weak smile. "Hi, little fellow," Lazarus said. The dog licked Lazarus in the face. Lazarus smiled and tried to rub the dog, but he was too weak. The dog lay down next to Lazarus, to keep him warm, and before Lazarus knew it, he had fallen asleep.

The next day, Lazarus awoke to three dogs keeping him warm. "Thank you for your mercy, God!" Lazarus said. "I knew I haven't been the man you wanted me to be, and for that, I'm sorry," Lazarus continued. Julius came out, screaming at the dogs to leave. "Get out of here!" he yelled. He knelt down to mock Lazarus. "I see you met a few friends," Julius mocked. "Julius, please give me something to eat," Lazarus pleaded. "I don't think so, Lazarus. Now, if you go to a shelter like I told you to, you could have a hot bath and a meal." "Why are you doing this?" Lazarus asked. "Because I hate you, Lazarus," Julius snapped. Julius covered his nose with his hand, because he couldn't stand the smell that was coming from Lazarus. "Julius, this is inhumane, even for you," Lazarus snapped. "Lazarus, I really don't care what you think. You deserve everything you're getting. You took Ava from me, and for that, you deserve the hell you're going through" Julius snapped. He went back into his million-dollar house. Lazarus lie there with tears streaming down his face. Lazarus then breathed his last breath.

The next morning, Marcus sat at the kitchen table, drinking coffee. Angela sat on the couch, playing with Lazarus' daughter. "So, you still haven't figured out where Lazarus could be?" Angela asked. "I haven't figured it out, but I have an idea of who does," Marcus said, sipping his coffee. "I don't understand," Angela said, confused. "When I went to Lazarus' house, some lady answered the door. She informed me that Lazarus no longer lives there and that they were under new management. When I asked who was the new owner, she said Julius," Marcus confessed. "Why that low down jerk!" Angela said, shaking her head. "I'm going to pay Julius a visit this morning and get some answers," Marcus said, grabbing a coat. "Well, we are coming with you. If you do find Lazarus, I think it's important that he sees his little girl," Angela said, wrapping the baby up and grabbing her coat. Marcus smiled at his wife and kissed her on the forehead. They headed out to confront Julius. When they arrived at Julius's house, Marcus let out a sigh. "Maybe you should stay in the car. This could get nasty," Marcus suggested. "No, Marcus, I want to see what he has to say," Angela argued. Marcus got out and opened the door for Angela and the baby. When they got closer to the house, Marcus noticed Lazarus lying lifeless on the porch. Angela began to cry, because it was very obvious that Lazarus was dead. Marcus ran over to him and tried to see if he was breathing, and when he discovered that he wasn't, he started CPR. "What is all this commotion?" Julius said, coming out. When he saw Lazarus lying there, dead, his mouth dropped opened. "Don't just stand there Julius, call for help!" Angela yelled.

Chapter 25

Angela held Lazarus' daughter close to her chest and got back in the car. Tears streamed down her face as she thought about Lazarus' lifeless body lying there. Soon, the paramedics arrived and Angela watched as if it was a scene from a movie. Marcus slowly walked over to the car. "What's going on?" Angela asked. "The paramedics just pronounced Lazarus dead. They are sending for the coroners. I want you to go home, you and the baby. This is no place for Liza to be," Marcus said. Angela knew better than to argue with her husband. She nodded her head and kissed her husband goodbye.

Later that day, after the paramedics and coroners left, Marcus sat there on the couch, speechless. Julius, however, seemed to be at peace. He poured himself some bourbon and began drinking. Marcus got up and walked over to his friend, as if he was in a trance. He looked at Julius as if he wanted to hit him. "What did you do?" Marcus cried. "I did nothing, Marcus. Lazarus brought this on himself," Julius snapped. "What?" Marcus said, in disbelief. "Look, Marcus, I told him to leave and he wouldn't," Julius said. "Julius, you took the man's home. Where was he supposed to go?" Marcus asked. "He could have gone to a shelter," Julius said, drinking his bourbon. Marcus knocked the glass out of his hand, shattering the glass all over the floor. "Is this a joke to you? A man is dead because of you and all you can do is make excuses," Marcus said, getting in his face. "Marcus, I did nothing wrong," Julius said, defending himself. "You really believe that, don't you Julius?" Marcus scoffed. Julius said nothing and there was a brief silence between the two. Marcus buried his face in his hands. Even after all that happened, he still loved his friend. Tears fell from his eyes as he thought about Julius' soul. "There is still time!" Marcus blurted out. "What?" Julius said, confused by Marcus outburst. "Julius, you still have time to repent. Ask God to forgive you for what you did to Lazarus. Please, before it is too late," Marcus said, grabbing him. "Let me go, Marcus," Julius said, snatching away. "I am not responsible for this," Julius argued. "Can't you see, Julius, that you have Lazarus' and Ava's blood on your hands? You are responsible! Can't you see the evil you've done? You did this, Julius," Marcus cried. "Lazarus deserved everything he got. I hope he and Ava are both rotting in hell," Julius said. "You don't mean that!" Marcus said, shaking his head. "I do mean it! As a matter of fact, for the first time in a long time, I am happy. I think I'll throw myself a party tonight," Julius said, smiling. Marcus looked at his friend and shook his head. "I pray for your soul," Marcus said. He grabbed his coat, looked back at his friend, and walked out.

Later that night, Julius had a celebration like he said he would. He was surrounded by friends and family. He had everything a person could possibly want: expensive food and wine, elegant decorations, and celebrities. Julius was the center of attention and he was having the time of his life. All of his friends and family admired him, others wanted to be him, and the women all wanted him. Julius danced the night away. He flirted with the women, but went over to hang with his brothers, John and Kevin. He sat there, feeling like he was on top of the world. All of a sudden, he began gasping for air. "Julius, what's wrong?" John asked. Julius said nothing, but passed out on the floor. Kevin immediately got on the floor to check Julius' breathing. "Call 911!" Kevin yelled to John. Julius couldn't speak, he just kept gasping for air, like a fish out of water. The music stopped and all the people watched in horror as Kevin tried to do CPR on his brother. Kevin tried until the paramedics came, and then they took over. They tried CPR as well, but Julius was already gone. Kevin and John both stood there, lost.

Days later, at the burial, John, Kevin, Marcus, and the rest of the family and friends gathered to say their goodbyes to Julius. It was one of the biggest funerals they'd ever seen. The preacher said a prayer and a few words about Julius' character. Everyone threw roses on his casket and slowly walked away. Everyone left but Marcus. He stood there, with tears flowing down his face. "Are you going to be alright, Marcus?" John asked. Marcus looked at John, but said nothing. Marcus just focused his attention on the closed casket. "Julius is in a better place now," John said. "No! No, he isn't, John," Marcus began. "What? What are you saying?" John asked. "My best friend is burning in hell!" Marcus blurted out. "Marcus, you are hysterical. Let me take you home," John insisted. "No! I can't go home! Can't you see, John? He is lost forever! He never accepted Jesus as his Lord and Savior!" Marcus said, crying. John tried grabbing his hysterical friend. "I tried, God! I tried to tell him the truth," Marcus said, crying. John grabbed his friend and held him in his arms. At that moment, John realized that Marcus was telling the truth and that he and his brothers had all been living a life of sin.

THE END!

A love-triangle that turns deadly. Ava is a woman trapped between two men. Julius is a rich and powerful man, with the world at his feet. While Lazarus is simply a hard-working man who comes into town and steals Ava's heart.

ANONNA REIGN is a gifted fiction author who is known for writing romance novels with a spiritual message. She lives in a small town in Illinois with her family.

Anonna's Journey started at a young age. She was inspired when she entered a school play and was selected as the narrator for the story in the play. She went on to write short stories that family and friends later encouraged her to pursue as a professional career.

Her debut novel, "Lazarus" received a five-star welcome and touching personal stories of faith and encouragement from her readers.

Anonna's writing style encourages her readers to explore a deeper walk with God. Her desire in writing is to spread faith, love, laughter, and awareness to her readers.

In addition to her novel, Anonna has a bachelor's degree in psychology. She's an advocate for autism and works with her elders as a caregiver.

When she's not writing Anonna enjoys spending time with family, gardening, watching movies, caring for her pets, attending her local church, and spending time outdoors.

Other books by Anonna Reign: The Therapist, My Sisters, and My Brother's Keeper.

Other books by Anonna Reign:
The Therapist, My Sisters, My Brother's Keeper

Quantum
Discovery
A LITERARY AGENCY

ISBN 978-1-961601-53-6

9 781961 601536

90000